"Do you know how incredibly perfect you are?"

Zane's hands wrapped around Jess's waist, and thrilling warmth heated her skin. "I'm not."

"You are. You can't let what those two did to you change who you are. That guy was the stupidest man on earth. You have every right to feel hurt, Jess. But don't let what he did change the person that you are."

"You think that's what I'm doing?"

"Isn't it? You changed your hair, your eyes. You dress differently now. Don't get me wrong, you look beautiful, sweetheart. But you were beautiful before."

She shrugged. She found it hard to believe.

"I needed the change." Tears misted in her eyes.

"I get that." Zane took her into his arms and hugged her, as a friend now. "But promise me one thing?"

"What?"

"Don't try to find what you need with another man. It makes me crazy."

* * *

Her Forbidden Cowboy is part of the Moonlight Beach Bachelors series—
Three men living in paradise...and longing for more.

* * *

If you're on Twitter, tell us what you think of Harlequin Desire! #harlequindesire

Dear Reader,

Welcome to my Moonlight Beach Bachelors series! We're starting off with a bang in *Her Forbidden Cowboy* with what I know best...cowboys! If you're an avid reader then you've already met Zane Williams, heartbroken country-and-western superstar who was introduced in *Redeeming the CEO Cowboy*.

Zane is recuperating from an injury on beautiful Moonlight Beach on the Southern California coastline. Away from what's familiar to him—his career and hometown—he's healing from physical and emotional wounds when his deceased wife's little sister comes calling. The next thing Zane knows, he's knee-deep in desire for Jessica Holcomb, the one woman on the planet who is forbidden to him.

BTW—don't you think Zane Williams is a great name for a country superstar? Think of a younger George Strait or present-day Luke Bryan. Yep, Zane is that appealing, and I actually fell in love with the name (and cowboy) when my nephew Zane William Pettis was born!

Keep an eye out for reclusive Adam Chase and sexy Dylan McKay in this first story. They will have their own trials and trouble with women on their way to HEA (happily-ever-after) coming in the next two installments of Moonlight Beach Bachelors!

So sit back, relax and enjoy a bit of sunshine on the shores of Moonlight Beach!

Happy reading!

Charlene Sands

HER FORBIDDEN COWBOY

CHARLENE SANDS

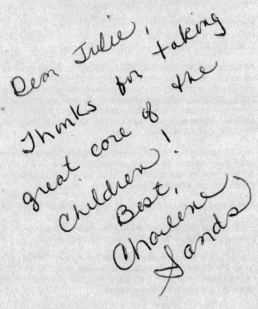

Dear Julie,
Thanks for taking
great care of the
children! Best,
Charlene Sands

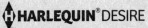

HARLEQUIN® DESIRE

ISBN-13: 978-0-373-73366-8

Her Forbidden Cowboy

Copyright © 2015 by Charlene Swink

Printed in U.S.A.

www.Harlequin.com

Charlene Sands is a *USA TODAY* bestselling author of more than thirty-five romance novels, writing sensual contemporary romances and stories of the Old West. Her books have been honored with a National Readers' Choice Award, a CataRomance Reviewers' Choice Award, and she's a double recipient of the Booksellers' Best Award. She belongs to the Orange County chapter and the Los Angeles chapter of RWA.

Charlene writes "hunky heroes with heart." She knows a little something about true romance—she married her high school sweetheart! When not writing, Charlene enjoys sunny Pacific beaches, great coffee, reading books from her favorite authors and spending time with her family. You can find her on Facebook and Twitter. Charlene loves to hear from her readers! You can write her at PO Box 4883, West Hills, CA 91308, or sign up for her newsletter for fun blogs and ongoing contests at charlenesands.com.

Books by Charlene Sands

Harlequin Desire

Visit the Author Profile page
at Harlequin.com for more titles.

To our own Zane William (Pettis), the bright little light in our family. And to his mommy, Angi, and daddy, Kent, with love to all!

One

The heels of Jessica's boots beat against the redwood of Zane Williams's sun-drenched deck overlooking the Pacific Ocean. Shielded by the shade of an overhang, he didn't miss a move his new houseguest made as he leaned forward on his chaise longue. His sister-in-law had officially arrived.

Was he still allowed to call her that?

Gusty breezes lifted her caramel hair, loosening the knot at the back of her head. A few wayward tendrils whipped across her eyes and, as she followed behind his assistant Mariah, her hand came up to brush them away. Late afternoon winds were strong on Moonlight Beach, swirling up from the shore as the sun lowered on the horizon. It was the time most sunbathers packed up their gear and went home and the locals came out. Shirt-billowing weather and one of the few things he'd come to like about California beach living.

He removed his sunglasses to get a better look at her. She wore a snowdrift-white blouse tucked into washed-to-the-millionth-degree jeans and a wide brown belt. Tortoiseshell-rimmed eyeglasses delicately in place didn't hide the pain and distress in her eyes.

Sweet Jess. Seeing her brought back so many memories, and the frigidness in his heart thawed a bit.

She looked like...*home.*

It hurt to think about Beckon, Texas. About his ranch

and the life he'd had there once. It hurt to think about how
he'd met Jessica's sister, Janie, and the way their small-
town lives had entwined. In one respect, the tragedy that
occurred more than two years ago might've been a lifetime
ago. In another, it seemed as if time was standing still. Either way, his wife, Janie, and their unborn child were gone.
They were never coming back. His mouth began to twitch.
An ache in the pit of his stomach spread like wildfire and
scorched him from the inside out.

He focused on Jessica. She carried a large tapestry suitcase woven in muted tones of gray and mauve and peach.
He'd given Janie and Jessica matching luggage three years
ago on their birthdays. It had been a fluke that both girls,
the only two offspring of Mae and Harold Holcomb, were
born on the same day, seven years apart.

Grabbing at the crutches propped beside his lounge chair,
Zane slowly lifted himself up, careful not to fall and break
his other foot. Mariah would have his head if he got hurt
again. His casted wrist ached like the devil, but he refused
to have his assistant come running every damn time he
wanted to get up. It was bad enough she'd taken on the extra
role of nursemaid. He reminded himself to have his business manager give Mariah a big fat bonus.

She halted midway on the deck, her disapproving gaze
dropping to his busted wrist and crutches before she shot
him a silent warning. "Here he is, Jessica." Mariah's peach-
pie voice was sweet as ever for his houseguest. "I'll leave
you two alone now."

"Thanks, Mariah," he said.

Her mouth pursed tight, she about-faced and marched
off, none too pleased with him.

Jessica came forward. "Still such a gentleman, Zane,"
she said. "Even on crutches."

He'd forgotten how much she sounded like Janie. Hearing her sultry tone stirred him up inside. But that's about
all Janie and Jessica had in common. The two sisters were

different in most other ways. Jess wasn't as tall as her sister. Her eyes were a light shade of green instead of the deep emerald that had sparkled from Janie's eyes. Jess was brunette, Janie blonde. And their personalities were miles apart. Janie had been a risk-taker, a strong woman who could hold her own against Zane's country-star fame, which might've intimidated a less confident woman. From what he remembered about Jess, she was quieter, more subtle, a schoolteacher who loved her profession, a real sweetheart.

"Sorry about your accident."

Zane nodded. "Wasn't much of an accident. More like stupidity. I lost focus and fell off the stage. Broke my foot in three places." He'd been at the Los Angeles Amphitheater, singing a silly tune about chasing ducks on the farm, all the while thinking about Janie. A video of his fall went viral on the internet. Everyone in country music and then some had witnessed his loss of concentration. "My tour's postponed for the duration. Can't strum a guitar with a broken wrist."

"Don't suppose you can."

She put down her luggage and gazed over the railing to the shore below. Sunlight glossed over deep steely-blue water as whitecaps foamed over wet sand, the tide rising. "I suppose Mama must've strong-armed you into doing this."

"Your mama couldn't strong-arm a puppy."

She whipped around to face him, her eyes sharp. "You know what I mean."

He did. Fact was, he wouldn't refuse Mae Holcomb anything. And she'd asked him this favor. *It's huge*, she'd said to him. *My Jess is hurtin' and needs to clear her head. I'm asking you to let her stay with you a week, maybe two. Please, Zane, watch out for her.*

He'd given his word. He'd take care of Jess and make sure she had time to heal. Mae was counting on him, and there wasn't anything he wouldn't do for Janie's mother. She deserved that much from him.

"You can stay as long as you like, Jess. You've got to know that."

Her mouth began to tremble. "Th-thanks. You heard what happened?"

"I did."

"I—I couldn't stay in town. I had to get out of Texas. The farther, the better."

"Well, Jess, you're as far west as you could possibly go." Five miles north of Malibu by way of the Pacific Coast Highway.

Her shoulders slumped. "I feel like such a fool."

Reaching out, he cupped her chin, forcing her eyes to his, the darn crutch under his arm falling to rest on the railing. "Don't."

"I won't be very good company," she whispered, dang near breathless.

His body swayed, not allowing him another unassisted moment. He released her and grabbed for his crutch just in time. He tucked it under his arm and righted his position. "That makes two of us."

Her soft laughter carried on the breeze. Probably the first bit of amusement she'd felt in days.

He smiled.

"I just need a week, Zane."

"Like I said, take as long as you need."

"Thanks." She blinked, and her eyes drifted down to his injuries. "Uh, are you in a lot of pain?"

"More like, I'm being a pain. Mariah's getting the brunt of my sour mood."

"Now I can share it with her." Her eyes twinkled for a second.

He'd forgotten what it was like having Jess around. She was ten years younger than him, and he'd always called her his little sis. He hadn't seen much of her since Janie's death. Cursed by guilt and anguish, he'd deliberately re-

CHARLENE SANDS   11

moved himself from the Holcombs' lives. He'd done enough damage to them.

"Hand up your luggage to me," he told her. With his good hand, he tucked his crutches under his armpits and propped himself, then wiggled his fingers. If he could get a grip on the bag...

Jessica rolled her eyes and hoisted her valise. "I appreciate it, Zane. But I've got this. Really, it's not heavy. I packed light. You know, summer-at-the-beach kind of clothes."

She let him off the hook. He would've tried, but fooling with her luggage wouldn't have been pretty. The doggone crutches made him clumsy as a drunken sailor, and he wasn't supposed to put any weight on his foot yet. "Fine, then. Why don't you settle in and rest up a bit? I'm bunking on this level. You've got an entire wing of rooms to yourself upstairs. Take your pick and spread out."

He followed behind as she made her way inside the wide set of light oak French doors leading to the living room. "Feel free to look around. I can have Mariah give you a tour."

"No, that's not necessary." She scanned over what she could see of the house, taking in the expanse—vaulted ceilings, textured walls, art deco interior and sleek contemporary furniture. He caught her vibe, sensing her confusion. What was Zane Williams, a country-western artist and a born and bred Texan, doing living on a California beach? When he'd leased this place with the option to buy, he told himself it was because he wanted a change. He was building Zane's on the Beach, his second restaurant in as many years, and he'd been offered roles in several Hollywood movies. He didn't know if he was cut out for acting, so the pending offers were still on the table.

She sent him an over-the-shoulder glance. "It's...a beautiful house, Zane."

His crutches supporting him, he sidled up next to her, seeing the house from her perspective. "But not *me*?"

"I guess I don't know what that is anymore."

"It's just a house. A place to hang my hat."

She gave his hatless head a glance. "It's a palace on the sea."

He chuckled. So much for his attempt at humble. The house was a masterpiece. One of three designed by the architect who lived next door. "Okay, you got me there. Mariah found the house and leased it on the spot. She said it would shake the cobwebs from my head. Had it awhile, but this is my first summer here." He leaned back, darting a glance around. "At least the humidity is bearable and it never seems to rain, so no threat of thunderstorms. The neighbors are nice."

"A good place to rest up."

"I suppose, if that's what I'm doing."

"Isn't it?"

He shrugged, fearing he'd opened up a can of worms. Why was he revealing his innermost thoughts to her? They weren't close anymore. He hardly knew Jessica as an adult, and yet they shared a deeply powerful connection. "Sure it is. Are you hungry? I can have my housekeeper make you—"

"Oh, uh…no. I'm not hungry right now. Just a bit tired from the trip. I'd better go upstairs before I collapse right here on your floor. Thanks for having a limo pick me up. And, well, thanks for everything, Zane."

She rose on her tiptoes, and the soft brush of her lips on his cheek squeezed something tight in his chest. Her hair smelled of summer strawberries, and the fresh scent lingered in his nose as she backed away.

"Welcome." The crutches dug into his armpits as they supported his weight. He hated the damn things. Couldn't wait to be free of them. "Just a suggestion, but the room to the right of the stairs and farthest down the hall has the best view of the ocean. Sunsets here are pretty glorious."

"I'll keep that in mind." Her quick smile was probably

meant to fake him out. She could pretend she wasn't hurting all that badly if she wanted to, but dark circles under her eyes and the pallor of her skin told the real story. He understood. He'd been there. He knew how pain could strangle a person until all the breath was sucked out. Hell, he'd lived it. Was still living it. And he knew something about Holcomb family pride, too.

What kind of jerk would leave any Holcomb woman standing at the altar?

Only a damn fool.

Jessica took Zane's advice and chose the guest room at the end of the hallway. Not for the amazing sunsets as Zane had suggested, but to keep out of his hair. Privacy was a precious commodity. He valued it, and so did she now. A powerful urge summoned her to slump down on the bed and cry her eyes out, but she managed to fight through the sensation. She was done with self-pity. She wasn't the first woman to be dumped at the altar. She'd been duped by a man she'd loved and trusted. She'd been so sure and missed all of the telling signs. Now she saw them through crystal clear eyes.

She busied herself unpacking her one suitcase, layering her clothes into a long, stylish light wood dresser. Carefully she set her jeans, shorts, swimsuits and undies into two of the nine drawers. She plucked out a few sleeveless sundresses and walked over the closet. With a slight tug, the double doors opened in a whoosh. The scents of cedar and freshness filled her nostrils as she gazed into a girl cave almost the size of her first-grade classroom back in Beckon. Cedar drawers, shoe racks and silken hangers were a far cry from the tiny drywalled closet in her one-bedroom apartment.

Deftly she scooped the delicate hangers under the straps of her dresses and hung them up. Next she laid her tennis shoes, flip-flops and two pairs of boots, one flat, one high-heeled, onto the floor just under her clothes. Her meager collection barely made a dent in the closet space. She closed the double doors and leaned against them. Then she took her first real glimpse at the view from her second-story bedroom.

"Wow." Breath tunneled from her chest.

Aqua seas and the sun-glazed sky made for a spectacular vista from the wide windows facing the horizon. She swallowed in a gulp of awe. Then suddenly, a strange bone-rattling feeling of loss hit her. She shivered as if assailed by a winter storm.

Why now? Why wasn't she reveling in the beauty surrounding her?

Nothing's beautiful. You lost your sister, her unborn baby and your fiancé.

"Would you like to go out onto the balcony?"

She whirled around, surprised to find Mariah, Zane's fortyish blonde assistant standing in the doorway. She'd worked for him since before he had married Janie. Jessica and Mariah's paths had crossed a few times since then. "Oh, hi." She glanced at the narrow glass door at the far end of the wall that led to the balcony. It was obviously situated there to keep from detracting from the room's sweeping view of the Pacific. "Thanks, but maybe later."

"Sure, you must be tired from the flight. Is there anything I can do for you?"

"I don't think so. I've unpacked. A shower and a nap and I'll be good to go."

Mariah smiled. "I'll be leaving for the day. Mrs. Lopez, Zane's housekeeper, is here. If you need anything, just ask her."

"Thank you… I'll be fine."

"Zane will want to have dinner with you. He eats dinner just before sunset. But he'd make an exception if you're hungry earlier."

"Sunset is fine."

Mariah studied her, her eyes unflinching and kind. "You look a little like Janie."

"I doubt that. Janie was beautiful."

"I see a resemblance. If you don't mind me saying, you have the same soulful eyes and lovely complexion."

She was pale as a ghost, and ten freckles dotted her nose. Yep, she'd counted them. Though, she'd never had acne or even a full-fledged zit to speak of in her teens. She supposed her complexion wasn't half-bad. "Thank you. I, uh, don't want to cause Zane or you any trouble. I'm basically here because it would've been harder to convince my mother otherwise, and I didn't want her to worry about me off in some deserted location to search my soul. Mama's had enough on her plate. She doesn't need to fret over me."

"I get it. Actually, you might be exactly what Zane needs to get his head out of the sand."

That was an odd statement. She narrowed her eyes, trying to make sense of it.

"He's not been himself for a while now," Mariah explained without spelling it out. Jessica gave her credit for the delicate way she put it.

"I figured. He lost his family. We all did," Jess said. She missed Janie something awful. Sometimes life was cruel.

Mariah nodded. "But having family around might be good for both of you."

She doubted that. She'd be a thorn in Zane's side. A kink in his plans. She would bide her time here, soak up some fresh sea air and then return home to face the music. Humiliation and desperate hurt had made her flee Texas. But she'd have to go back eventually. Her face pulled tight. She didn't want to think about that right now.

"Maybe," she said to Mariah.

"Well, have a good evening."

"Thanks. You, too."

After Mariah left, Jessica plucked up her shampoo and entered the bathroom. Oh, boy, and she'd thought the closet was something. The guest bathroom came equipped with a television, a huge oval Jacuzzi tub and an intricately tiled spacious shower that was digitized for each of the three shower heads looming above. She peered closer to read the monitor. She could program the time, temperature and force of the shower and heaven knew what else.

After she punched in a few commands, the shower spurted to life, and water rained down. Jess smiled. A new toy. Peeling off her clothes, she opened the clear glass door and stepped inside. Steamy spray hit her from three sides, with two heads spewing softly and one pulsing like the pumping of her heart. She turned around and around, using the fragrant liquid soap from a dispenser in the wall. She lingered there, lost in the mist and jet stream as pent-up tension seeped out of her bones, her limbs loose and free. Eventually, she got down to business and worked shampoo into her hair. Much too early, the shower turned off automatically. As she stepped out, the steam followed her. She dried herself with a cushy white towel. How nice.

She dressed in a pair of tan midthigh shorts and a cocoa-brown tank top. She hoped dinner with Zane wasn't a formal thing. She hadn't brought anything remotely fashionable.

After blow-drying her hair, she lifted the long strands up in a ponytail, leaving bangs to rest on her forehead. A little nap had sounded wonderful minutes ago, but now she was too keyed up to sleep. The time change would probably hit her like a ton of bricks later, but right now, the sandy wind-blown beach below beckoned her. She slipped her feet into flip-flops and headed downstairs.

Lured by the scent of spices and sauce wafting to her nose, she headed in that direction. Inside a magnificent granite-and-stone kitchen, she came face to face with an older woman, a little hefty in the hips, wearing an apron and humming to herself.

The woman turned around. "*Hola*, Miss Holcomb?"

"Yes, I'm Jessica."

"*Hola*, Jessica." She nodded. "I'm Mrs. Lopez. Do you like enchiladas?"

She was Texan. She loved everything Mexican. "Yes. Smells yummy."

Mrs. Lopez lowered the oven door, and a stainless-steel rack automatically pushed forward.

"They will be ready in half an hour. Can I get you a drink? Or a snack?"

"No, thank you. I'll wait for Zane. Well, it's nice to meet you," she said, retreating from the kitchen. "I'll be back in—"

A boom sounded. "Double damn you!" Zane's loud curse echoed throughout the house.

Jessica froze in place.

Mrs. Lopez grinned and shook her head. "He cannot dress himself too well. He will not let anyone help him. He is not such a good patient."

They shared a smile. "I see." But when she'd first arrived, he was wearing jeans and a casual cotton shirt. Was he dressing up now? "Do I need to change my clothes for dinner?"

"No, no. Mr. Zane spilled iced tea on his shirt. You are dressed nice."

"Thank you." Okay, great. She felt better now. When she'd packed her clothes, she hadn't given much thought to her wardrobe. All she hoped for was to clear her head a little while here. "I thought I'd go for a walk on the beach. I'll be back in plenty of time for dinner. See you later."

Mrs. Lopez nodded and focused on the stove. Jess's stomach grumbled as she left the spicy smells of the kitchen and walked out the double doors to the deck. From there, she climbed a few more stairs down, until warm sand crept onto her flip-flops.

There were no lakes or rivers back home that compared with the balmy breezes whipping at her hair, the briny taste on her lips or the glistening golden hues reflecting off the ocean. Her steps fell lightly, making a slight impression in the packed wet sand until the next wave inched up the shore and carried her footprints out to sea. Even with the sun low over the water's edge, her skin warmed as she walked along the beach. To her right, beachfront mansions overlooking the sea filled her line of vision, each one different in design and structure. She was so intent on gauging the houses, she didn't notice a jogger approaching until he'd stopped right in front of her.

"Hi," he said, his breaths heaving.

"Hello." A swift glance at his face made her gasp silently. He was stunning and tanned and one of the most famous movie stars in the world. Dylan McKay.

He hunched over, hands on knees, catching his breath. "Give me a sec."

For what? She wanted to ask, yet she stood there, feet implanted in the sand, waiting. He was easy on the eyes, and she tried not to stare at his bare chest and the dip of his jogging shorts below a trim waist.

He righted his posture, and blood drained from her body as he aimed a heart-melting smile her way. "Thank you."

Puzzled, she stared at him. "For?"

"Being here. For giving me an excuse to stop running." He chuckled, and white teeth flashed. Was the sun-gleaming twinkle from his smile real? Could've been. Dylan McKay was every red-blooded woman's idea of the perfect man.

Except hers. She knew there was no such thing.

"Okay. But…you could've just stopped on your own, couldn't you?"

He shook his head. "No, I'm supposed to run ten miles a day. It's a work thing. I'm preparing for a role as a Navy SEAL."

No kidding? She wasn't going to pretend she didn't know who he was. Or that his bronzed body wasn't already honed and ripped. "Gotcha. How many did you do?"

His lips twisted with self-loathing. "Eight."

"That's not bad." Judging by the pained look on his face, he was a man who expected perfection of himself. "There aren't too many people who can run eight miles."

His expression lightened and he seemed to appreciate her encouragement. "I'm Dylan, by the way." He put out his hand.

"Jessica." It was a one-pump handshake.

"Are we neighbors?" he asked, his brows gathering. "I live over there." He pointed to a trilevel mansion looming close by.

She shook her head. "Not really. I'm staying with Zane Williams for a short time."

When his brows lifted ever so slightly and his eyes flashed, she read his mind. "He's…he's *family*."

He nodded. "I know Zane. Good guy."

"He is. My sister…well, he was married to Janie."

A moment passed as he put two and two together. "I'm sorry about what happened."

"Thank you."

"Well, I think I've gotten my second wind. Thanks to you. Only two miles to go. Nice meeting you, Jessica. Say hi to Zane for me."

He about-faced, trotted down the beach in the opposite direction and soon picked up his pace to a full-out jog.

She headed back to the house, a smile on her lips, a song humming in her heart. Maybe coming here wasn't such a bad idea after all.

She spotted Zane braced against the patio railing and waved. Had he been watching her? She was hit with a surge of self-consciousness. She wasn't a beach babe. Her curvy figure didn't allow two-piece bathing suits, and her pale skin tone could be compared only with the bark of a birch tree or the peel of a honeydew melon.

As she climbed the stairs, her gaze hit upon his shirt, a Hawaiian print with repeating palm trees. She'd never seen

Zane look more casual and yet appear so ill at ease in his surroundings.

"Nice walk?" he asked, removing his sunglasses.

"It beats a stroll to Beckon's Cinema Palace."

Zane laughed, a knowing glint in his eyes. "You got that right. I haven't thought about the Palace in a long time." His voice sounded gruff as if he'd go back to those days in a heartbeat.

There wasn't a whole lot to do in Beckon, Texas, so on Saturday night the parking lot at the Palace swarmed with kids from the high school. Hanging out and hooking up. It's where Jessica had had her first awkward kiss. With Miles Bernardy. Gosh, he was such a geek. But then, so was she.

It was also where Janie and Zane had fallen in love.

"I met one of your neighbors."

"Judging by the glow on your face, must've been Dylan. He runs this time of day."

"My face is not glowing." She blinked.

"Nothing to worry over. Happens all the time with women."

"I'm not a wom—I mean, I am not gawking over a movie star, for heaven's sake."

He should talk. Former brother-in-law or not, Zane Williams was a country superstar hunk. Dark-haired, six foot two, a chiseled-jawed Grammy winner, Zane wasn't hard on the eyes, either. The tabloids painted him as an eligible widower who needed love in his life. So far, they'd been kind to him, a rare thing for a superstar.

He picked up his crutches and lifted one to gesture to a table. "This okay with you?"

Two adjacent places were set along a rectangular glass table large enough for ten. Votive candles and a spray of flowers accented the place settings facing the sunset. "It's nice, Zane. I hope you didn't go to too much trouble. I don't expect you to entertain me."

"Not going to any trouble, Jess. Fact is, I eat out here

most days. I hate being cooped up inside the house. Just another week and I'll be out of these dang confinements." He raised his wrapped wrist.

"That's good news. Then what will you do?"

Inclining his head, he considered her question. "Some rehab, I'm told. And continue working out details on the restaurant." He frowned, and the light dimmed in his eyes. "My tour's not due to pick up until September sometime. *Maybe*."

She wouldn't pry about the maybe. He hobbled to the table. Leaning a crutch against the table's edge, he managed to pull out her chair—such chivalry—and she took her seat. Then he scooted his butt into his own chair. Plop. Poor Zane. His injuries put him completely out of his element.

Mrs. Lopez appeared with platters of food. She set them on the table with efficient haste and nodded to him. "I made a pitcher of margaritas to go with the enchiladas and rice. Or maybe some iced tea or soda?"

"Jessica?" he asked.

"A margarita sounds like heaven."

He glanced at the housekeeper. "Bring the pitcher, please."

She nodded. Within a minute, a pitcher appeared along with two bottle-green wide-rimmed margarita glasses. "Thanks," he said. Zane leaned forward and gripped the pitcher with his wrapped hand. His face pinched tight as he struggled to upend the weighty pitcher. He sighed, and she sensed his frustration over not being able to perform the simple task of pouring a drink with his right hand.

"Let me help," she said softly.

She slipped her hand under the pitcher and helped guide the slushy concoction into the glasses. She gave him credit for clamping his mouth shut and not complaining about his limitations.

"Thanks," he said. He reached out, and the slide of his rough fingers over hers sent warm tingles to her heart. They were still connected through Janie, and she valued his friendship now. She'd made the right decision in coming here.

The food was delicious. She inhaled the meal, emptying her plate within minutes. "I guess I didn't know how hungry I was. Or thirsty."

She reached for her second margarita and took a long sip. Tart icy goodness slid down her throat. "Mmm."

The sun had set with a parfait of swirling color, and now half the moon lit the night. The beach was quiet and calm. The roar of the waves had given way to an occasional lulling swish.

Zane sipped his third margarita. She remembered that about him. He could hold his liquor.

"So what are your plans now, Jess?" he asked.

"Hit the beach, work on my tan and stay out of your way. Shouldn't be too hard. The place is huge."

Tiny lines crinkled around his eyes, and he chuckled. "You don't need to stay out of my way. But feel free to do whatever you want. There are two cars parked in the garage, fueled and ready to go. I can't drive them."

"So how do you get around?"

"Mariah, usually. When I'm needed at the restaurant site or somewhere, she's drives me or I hire a car. She's been a trouper, going above and beyond since my accident."

Mrs. Lopez picked up the empty dishes, leaving the margarita pitcher. A smart woman.

"Thank you, Mrs. Lopez. Have a good night," Zane said. "See you tomorrow."

"Good night," she said to both of them.

"Thanks for the delicious enchiladas."

On a humble nod and smile, she exited the patio.

Zane pointed to her half-empty glass. "How many of those can you handle, darlin'?"

"Oh, uh…I don't know. Why?"

"'Cause if you fall flat on your face, I won't be able to pick you up and carry you to your room."

He winked, and a sudden vision of Zane carrying her to the bedroom burst into her mind. It wasn't as weird a notion as she might've thought. She felt safe with Zane. She truly liked him and didn't buy into his guilt over Janie's death. He wasn't to blame. He couldn't have known about faulty wiring in the house or the fire that would claim her life. Janie had loved Zane for the man that he was, had always been. She wouldn't want Zane's guilt to follow him into old age.

"Well, then, we're even. If you got pie-eyed, I wouldn't be able to pick you up, either." She took another long sip of her drink. Darn, but it tasted good. Her spirits lifted. Let the healing begin.

Zane cocked a crooked smile. "I like your style, *Miss Holcomb.*"

"Ugh. To think I would've been Mrs. Monahan by now. Thank God I'm not."

"The guy's an ass."

"Thanks for saying that. He sure had me fooled. Up until the minute I was having my bridal veil pinned in my hair, I thought I knew what the future had in store for me. I saw myself married to a man I had a common bond with. He was a high school principal. I was a grade-school teacher. We both loved education. But I was too blind to see that Steven had commitment phobia. He'd had one broken relationship after another before we started dating. I invested three years of my life in the guy, and I thought surely he'd gotten over it. I thought I was the one. But he was fooling himself as well as me." A pent-up breath whooshed out of her. A little bit of tequila loosened her tongue, and out poured her heart. The unburdening was liberating. "My friend Sally said Steven looked up his old girlfriend seeking sympathy after the wedding that never happened. Can you imagine?"

Zane stared at her. "No. He should be on his knees begging you for forgiveness. He did one thing right. He didn't marry you and make your life miserable. I hate to say it, darlin', but you're better off without him. The man doesn't deserve you. But you're hurt right now, and I get that. You probably still love him."

"I don't," she said, hoisting her glass and swallowing a big gulp. "I pretty much hate him."

Zane leaned back in his seat, his gaze soft on her. "Okay. You hate him. He's out of your life."

She braced folded elbows on the table and rested her chin on her hands. The sea was black as pitch now, the sky lit only with a few stars and clouded moonlight. "I just wanted…I wanted what you and Janie had. I wanted that kind of love."

Her fuzzy brain cleared. Oh, no. She hadn't just said that? She whipped her head around. Zane's expression of sympathy didn't change. He didn't flinch. He simply stared out to sea. "We had something pretty special."

"You did. I'm sorry for bringing it up."

"Don't be." His tone held no malice. "You're Janie's sister. You have as much right to talk about her as I do."

Tears misted in her eyes. "I miss her."

"I miss her, too."

She sighed. She didn't mean to put such a somber mood on the evening. Zane was gracious enough to allow her to stay here. She didn't want to bring him down. It was definitely time to call it a night. She put on a cheery face. "Well, this has been nice."

She rose, and her head immediately clouded up. The table, the railing, the ocean blurred before her. She batted her eyes over and over, trying to focus. Two Zanes popped into her line of vision. She reached for the tabletop, struggling to remain upright on her own steam. She swayed back and forth, unable to keep her body still. "Zane?"

"It just hit you, didn't it?"

"Oh, yeah. I think so." She giggled.

"Don't move for a second."

"I'll…try." A tornado swirled in her head. "Why?"

He rose and hobbled over to her. Using one crutch, he

tucked it under his left arm. "I'm going to help you get inside."

"But, you said…you c-couldn't. Uh…" She giggled again.

Zane wrapped his right arm around her shoulder. "Okay, now, darlin', I've got you. Your body will be my other crutch. We'll help each other. Move slowly."

"W-where are we g-going?"

"I've got to get you to bed."

Her head fell to his shoulder. Somewhere in the back of her mind, she thought how nice it felt to have him hold her. He smelled good. He would take care of her.

"Focus on putting one foot in front of the other."

She tried.

"That's good, honey."

Hobble-hopping, they moved together. It seemed to take forever to go a short distance in the dark shadows of the night. Keeping her eyes down, she watched her feet move. Then blinding light appeared in a burst. She squinted. "What's that?"

"We're inside the house now," Zane was saying.

"That's g-good, right? I'll be in b-bed soon." A warm buzz spread through her like soft, sweet jelly.

"Not upstairs. You'll never make it. We're going to my room."

She couldn't wait to lay her head down someplace. She didn't care where. More careful steps later, they entered a room. A ray of moonlight beamed like an arrow, aiming straight at the bed.

"Okay, we made it," Zane said. He sounded weird and out of breath. "You'll sleep here tonight."

He guided her down. The bed hit her bottom quickly and cushioned around her. She swayed sideways and was immediately set to right. Zane held her steady as the mattress dipped again and he sat next to her. Dizzying waves bombarded her head. She'd sat too quickly.

"Think you can take it from here?" he whispered.

No. Aware of Zane's eyes on her, she waited until the twister in her head calmed. "Yeah, I think so."

"Good."

Her giddiness fading, her lighthearted high dropped to a pitiful low. It hadn't taken her long to become a burden to Zane. If only she hadn't sucked down that second margarita. Zane had warned her to go slowly. Expensive tequila and jet lag had done her in. Man, chalk another mistake up to her lousy intuition.

"I'm sorry."

"Nothing to be sorry for," he said.

But she was, and an urge to thank him wiggled through the fog in her head. Pursing her lips, she leaned forward toward his cheek. Her aim off, she missed and caught the corner of his mouth instead. As she brushed a soft kiss there, he tasted of tequila and the sea. So good. Inside, a warm sprinkling of something wonderful spread through her body. "Thank you," she whispered, not sure if her words slurred.

Then his arms wrapped around her and gently lowered her down. Her head was enveloped in a large, fluffy pillow, and a silky sheet came to rest over her body.

She heard a whispered, "Welcome," right before the world finally stopped spinning.

Two

Jessica gazed at the digital clock on the nightstand. Eight-thirty! She flashed back to last night and drinking those two giant margaritas, then slowly looked around. She was in an unfamiliar bed.

She'd finally let go and given herself permission to have a good time, and where had that gotten her? She'd made a fool of herself. Zane had hobbled her inside the house and slept heaven only knew where. Was there another bedroom on this floor? Maybe a servant's quarters? She'd seen an office, a screening room and a game room. No beds, just couches. "Oh, man," she mumbled.

She scanned the stark but stylish bedroom where she'd slept. A flat-screen TV, a dresser and a low fabric sofa were the only other furniture in the room. If it wasn't for a shelf that housed Zane's five Grammys, as well as a couple of CMA and ACM awards, she wouldn't have guessed it was his master suite. There was nothing personal, warm and cozy about the space.

Hitching her body forward, she waited for signs of pain, but there was nothing. Thank goodness—no hangover. She grabbed her glasses from the nightstand, tossed off the covers and rose. Seeing she was still dressed in her shorts and tank top, she emitted a low groan from her throat as she slipped her feet into her flip-flops. How reckless of her. She'd abused Zane's hospitality already.

She entered the bathroom, another ode to magnificence, and glanced at herself in the mirror. Smudged mascara and rumpled hair reflected back at her. She washed her face and finger-combed her long wayward tresses. She'd take care of the rest once she reached her own room.

Exiting Zane's room, she made her way down a short hallway. Voices coming from the kitchen perked up her ears.

Mrs. Lopez spotted her and waved her inside. "Just in time for breakfast."

Mariah and Zane sat at the kitchen table, coffee mugs piping hot in front of them. Upon the housekeeper's announcement, both heads lifted her way. Blood rushed up her neck, and her face flamed.

"Morning," Zane said, peering into her eyes and not at her wrinkled mess of clothes. "You ready for some breakfast?"

"Good morning, Jessica," Mariah said. They'd obviously been deep in concentration, poring over a stack of papers.

"Yes, yes. Sit down," Mrs. Lopez insisted.

"Oh, uh…good morning. I don't want to intrude. You look busy."

"Just same old, same old," Mariah said. "We're going over plans for Zane's new restaurant. We could use your input."

She'd given Zane her input last night. God. She'd kissed him. Remembering that kiss sent a warm rash of heat through her body. She'd missed his cheek and gotten hold of his lips. Was it the alcohol, or had her heart strummed from that kiss? The alcohol. Had to be. He must have known it was a genuine miscalculation on her part. She hadn't meant to kiss him that way.

"Yes, have a seat, Jess," he said casually. "You need to eat. And we sure need a fresh perspective."

Before her shower? Luckily Zane hadn't mentioned anything about her lack of discretion last night or her state of dress today. She'd overslept, that much was a given. Back home, she rose before six every morning. She loved to go through the morning newspaper, take a walk in the backwoods and then eat a light breakfast before heading to her classroom.

There were a platter of bagels with cream cheese, a scrambled egg jalapeno dish and cereal boxes on the table. The eggs smelled heavenly, and her stomach grumbled. Seeing no other option, she sat down and reached for the eggs as Mrs. Lopez provided her with a bowl and a cup of coffee.

"Bien." She gave a satisfied nod.

Jessica smiled at her.

As Zane and his assistant finished up their breakfast, she ate, too, complimenting Mrs. Lopez on the food she'd prepared.

Zane told Mariah, "Janie and Jessica worked at their folks' café in Beckon. They served the best fried chicken in all of Texas."

"That's what most folks said," she agreed. She couldn't claim modesty. Her parents *did* make the best fried chicken in the state. "My parents opened Holcomb House when I was young. They worked hard to make a go of it. It wasn't anything as grand as what you're probably planning, but in Beckon, the Holcomb House was known for good eats and a friendly atmosphere. When Dad died five years ago, my mom couldn't make a go of it by herself. I think she lost the will, so she sold the restaurant. I'm no expert, but if I can help in any way, I'll give it a try."

"Great," Mariah said.

"Appreciate it," Zane added. "This restaurant will be a little different than the one in Reno, in cuisine and atmosphere. The beach is a big draw for tourists, and we want it to be a great experience."

Zane probably had half a dozen financial advisors, but if he needed her help in any way, she'd oblige. How could she not? She cringed thinking that Zane slept on a sofa last night. A quick glance at his less than crisp clothes, the same clothes he'd worn last night, meant that he probably hadn't got to shower this morning, either. Because of her.

Once the dishes were cleared, Mariah pushed a few papers over to her. "If you don't mind, could you tell us what you think of the menu? Are the prices fair? Do the titles of the dishes make sense? We're working with a few chefs and want to get it just right. These are renderings of what Zane's on the Beach will look like once all done, exterior and interior."

For the next hour, Jessica worked with the two of them, giving her opinion, voicing her concerns when they probed and offering praise honestly if not sparingly. Zane's on the Beach had everything a restaurant could offer. Outside, patio tables facing the beach included a sand bar for summer nights of drinking under the moonlight. Inside, window tables were premium, with the next row of tables raised to gain a view of the ocean, as well. It wasn't posh, but it wasn't family dining, either. "I like that you've made it accessible to a younger crowd. The prices are fair. Have you thought about putting a little stage in the bar? Invite in local entertainment to perform?"

Mariah shot a look at Zane. "We discussed it. I think it's a great idea. Zane isn't so sure."

Zane scrubbed his chin, deep in thought. "I've got to get a handle on what I want from this restaurant. My name and reputation are at stake. Do I want ocean views and great food or a hot spot for a younger crowd?"

"Why can't you have both?" Jessica asked. "Quality is quality. Diners will come for the cuisine and ambiance. After hours, the place can transform into a nightspot for the millennials."

Amused, Zane's dark eyes sparked. "Millennials? Are you one?"

"I guess so."

His head tilted, and his mouth quirked up. "Why do I suddenly feel old?"

"Because you are," Mariah jabbed. "You're cranking toward forty."

"Thirty-five is a far shot from forty, and that's all I'm saying."

"You're wise to stop there," Mariah said playfully, yet with a note of warning. Jessica could tell that Mariah Jacobellis wasn't a woman who put up with age jokes. Although Mariah was physically lovely, she seemed to take no prisoners when it came to business or her personal life. Jessica admired that about her. Maybe she could take a lesson from her rule book.

Zane leaned way back in his seat. "You got that right."

Mariah stacked the papers on the table and rose, hugging them to her chest. "Well, I'm off to make some phone calls. Zane, think about when you want to resume your tour. I've got to let the event coordinators know. They're on my back about it. Oh, and be sure to read through that contract that Bernie sent over the other day."

Zane's lips pursed. "I'll do my best."

"Jessica, have a nice morning. And if you're around Zane today, please give him a hand. He may look like a superhero, but he's really not Superman."

Could've fooled her. Last night, he'd been super *heroic*.

Mariah pivoted on her heels and strode out the door.

Zane chuckled.

"What?"

"The look on your face."

"I'm mortified about last night. Where on earth did you sleep, and does Mariah know what happened?"

"First off, don't be upset. It's our little secret. Mariah doesn't know that you're a margarita lightweight." He smiled. "That woman's been babying me for weeks. Doesn't do a man a bit of good being so dang useless. For the first time in a month of Sundays, I was able to help out and do something useful with this banged-up body."

"I took your bed."

"Glad to give it up."

"Where did you sleep?"

"The office sofa is the most comfortable place in the whole house."

"Oh, boy. I'm sorry. The first night I'm here, I give you trouble."

He smiled again, a stunning heart-melter. "If livening up my life some is trouble, then bring it on. Fact is, I'm glad you're here. You bring a bit of home with you. I miss that."

She needed to believe him. She'd been afraid coming here would remind him of Janie and all that he'd lost. To have him say he was glad she'd come made a big difference. "Okay."

He put his palms on her cheeks and leaned forward. Her heart stopped. Was he going to kiss her? His touch sent tingles parading up and down her chest. Oh, wow. It wasn't alcohol this time. Probably wasn't the alcohol last night, either. She'd been dumped by a scoundrel, and now a man she had no right responding to made her feel giddy inside. How screwed up was that?

She gazed into his eyes. He was looking somewhere above her eyeglasses. Then he lowered his mouth—she stilled—and he brushed a brotherly kiss across her forehead. Breath eased from her chest, and her foolish heart tumbled. Of course, Zane wasn't going to kiss her *that* way.

"And thanks for the input about the restaurant," he said. "I respect your honesty and what you have to offer."

She swallowed hard. Tamping down her silly emotions, she offered a quick smile. "Anytime."

Beaming sunshine simmered over Jessica's body, the invading heat soaking into her bones. Salty air, a cushion of sand beneath her and the soothing sounds of waves crashing upon the shore gave her good reason to forget her disastrous relationship with Steven Monahan. He didn't deserve any more of her time. But the sting of his rejection stayed with her, leaving her hollowed out inside, afraid to trust, questioning her intuition. She feared she'd never fully recover the innocence of her first love. Good thing she didn't have to make any decisions here on Moonlight Beach. She could just be.

Drenched in sunscreen, she lay on a beach blanket in a modest one-piece bathing suit, a folded towel under her head. Slight breezes just outside Zane's beachfront home deposited flecks of sand onto her arms and legs. Children's giggles and adult conversations drifted to her ears. For the first time in days, her nerves were completely calm.

She promised herself to keep out of Zane's hair, and she had for the most part these past three days. He spent hours inside his office working with Mariah, and occasionally they would ask for her input on the restaurant. She figured it was just a way for him to keep her entertained and make her feel welcome. Each morning, under an overcast sky that would burn off before noon, she walked a three-mile stretch of beach, loosening up her limbs and clearing her head. At night, she'd dine with Zane on the patio facing the ocean, and except for having an occasional glass of white wine or a cold beer, she kept her alcohol consumption to a bare minimum. The Pacific Ocean and fresh air were her balm. She didn't need to rely on anything else.

She wiggled her tush into the sand, carving out a more comfy spot on her blanket, and closed her eyes. The flapping of wings and piercing squawk of a seagull overhead made her smile.

"Glad to see you've taken to Moonlight Beach."

Blocking rays of sunlight with a hand salute, she opened her eyes. The handsome face of Dylan McKay came into view.

"Hi, Jessica." He stared at her with his million-dollar smile. "Don't let me disturb you."

Gosh, he remembered her name.

Wearing plaid board shorts and a muscle-hugging white

T-shirt, and fitting into beach society with the casualness of a megastar, he sort of did disturb her. Yet he did so in such a friendly way, she didn't mind the intrusion. As she sat up on her elbows, his gaze dipped to her chest. To his credit, his eyes didn't linger on her breasts, and that was more than she could say about most men.

"Hello, and I am enjoying the beach. When in Rome, as they say." She chuckled at the cliché. It was Mama's favorite saying, and she'd used it a zillion times over the years. The most recent was last night when they'd talked on the phone. Did others in her generation get that phrase?

Her eyes fell on a black portfolio tucked under his arm. It looked odd there, as if he should be wearing a three-piece suit while carrying that austere leather case. Instead of moving on, he squatted down beside her, his tanned knees nearly in her face. Obviously, he wanted to chat.

"I see you sometimes in the morning, walking along the beach."

"You've inspired me," she said. "Of course, I only do three miles. How are your runs going?"

"Killing me, but I'm getting in the ten miles."

His legs were taut, like those of a natural runner, and the rest of his body, well…it would be hard not to notice his muscles and the way his T-shirt nearly split at the seams around his shoulders and upper arms. "Good for you."

"So, how's it going?" he asked. "Other than sunbathing and taking long walks, are you having a good time?"

"Yes. It's nice here. I'm working on some new lesson plans for my class. I teach first grade back home."

"Ah…a teacher. Such an honorable profession."

She waggled her brows. Was he poking fun at her? Or was he being genuine?

"My mother taught school for thirty-five years," he added, his smile wistful, pride filling his voice. "She was loved by her students, but she wasn't a pushover. It wasn't easy pulling my antics on her. She was too savvy. She knew when kids were up to no good."

"I bet you gave her a run for her money."

He laughed, the gleam of his lake-blue eyes touching her. "I did."

"What grade did she teach?"

"All grades, but she preferred fourth and fifth. Then, later on, she became dean of a middle school, and eventually, the principal of the high school."

She nodded. She didn't have much else to add to the conversation. Not that Dylan McKay wasn't easy to talk to. He was. And she loved talking about education to anyone who would listen. It was just that he was fabulous, famous Dylan McKay. And he kept smiling at her.

"Hey, I'm having a party on Saturday night. If you're still here, I'd love for you to come. Maybe you can get Zane to get out and have a little fun."

"Oh, thanks." He'd caught her off guard. Wasn't that what she needed right now, to be a wallflower at an A-list party? "I'm…uh, I'm not the partying type. Especially now."

"Now?"

She shrugged. "I'm going through something and need a little R and R."

"Ah…a breakup?"

She nodded. Her pride aside, she opened up a little to make her point. "Broken engagement as the wedding guests were taking their seats in church."

"Ah…gotcha. I've been there once, a long time ago, when I was too young to know better. It turned out for the best, so believe me, I understand. Listen, I promise you, the party is low-key. Just a few friends and neighbors for a barbecue on the beach. I'd love to see you there."

"Thanks."

He smiled, and she smiled back. Then he pointed to her upper thigh, on the right side, closest to him. "Uh-oh. Looks like you missed a spot. You're starting to burn."

Grabbing the sunscreen tube from the blanket, his long fingers brushed the soft underside of her hand as he set the sunscreen into her palm. "Better lather up and—"

"Stop corrupting my little sis, McKay."

Jessica whipped her head around. Zane stood on the sundeck railing, staring at Dylan. His voice was a far cry from menacing, but the cool look he shot Dylan made her wonder what was up.

Dylan winked at her. "Maybe she wants to be corrupted."

"And maybe you want to turn tail and go home. I don't have to read that script, you know."

"Whoops," he said, flashing a charming smile. "He's got me there. Maybe you can help me convince him to take this role. Wanna try? Since you're about to turn into a fried tomato out here."

Under normal circumstances, she was probably the least starstruck person in Beckon, Texas, but how could she not take Dylan up on his offer to go over a movie script? The notion got her juices flowing, and excitement buzzed around her like a busy little bee.

She glanced down at her legs. Oh, wow. Dylan was right. There were more than a few splotchy patches on her body. Time to get out of the sun. "Sure, why not?"

"Great." He swiveled his head in Zane's direction. "We're coming up right now."

Gallantly, he offered her his hand. She couldn't very well refuse the gesture. She slipped one hand into his and simultaneously clutched her cover-up with the other as they rose together. He was too close for comfort, his eyes smiling on her, their hands entwined. Gently she pulled away, making herself busy zipping herself into a white cotton cover up and ignoring his rapt attention. He was a charmer, but thankfully his touch hadn't elicited a jolt of any kind. She glanced at Zane, leaning by the railing, his sharp gaze fixed on her. Something hot and unruly sizzled in the pit of her belly.

She ignored it and pushed on, climbing the steps with Dylan McKay following behind.

"Did he ask you out?" Zane probed the minute Dylan McKay exited the house. Looming over her, Zane was a bit foreboding, as if he was her white knight protecting her from the wicked prince of darkness. Geesh.

"Wh-what?"

"The guy couldn't take his eyes off you down on the beach."

She shrugged and picked up three empty glasses, reminiscent of her waitress days at Holcomb House.

After coming back into the house she'd left the two men to take a quick shower and slip on a sundress. She'd listened to Dylan's script proposal to Zane with keen interest in a spacious light oak–paneled office on the main level of the house. The meeting took almost an hour. Then they'd had drinks in the cool shade of the patio. Iced tea for her. The men were content to knock back whiskey and soda.

Dylan was a charming lady's man to the millionth degree, and she knew enough to steer clear. The idea that he'd be interested in a little ol' school teacher from Beckon, Texas, was ridiculous. She had no illusions of anything else going on between them, and Zane should know that.

Her mama's image flashed before her eyes. That was it. She bet her mother put Zane up to watching out for her, making sure her tender heart didn't get broken again. Well, heck. She'd let him off the hook, but not without giving him some grief. Her chin up, she said, "He invited me to his beach party Saturday night. It was just a friendly invitation."

Zane's mouth tightened into a snarl and he snorted. "Doubtful."

"I told him I probably wouldn't go."

"Good." Zane nodded, satisfied. "You don't need to get involved with him. He's—"

"Out of my league?"

His eyes widened. "Hell, no."

"Well, he is. And I know it all too well. Heck, my life is messy enough right now. There's no room for romance, though it's absurd to think of Dylan McKay actually being into me."

Zane immediately reached out to grab her arm. Surprised, she jerked from his touch, and the glasses she held nearly slipped from her hand. "Don't put yourself down, Jess."

A jolt sprang to life, spiraling out of control where the strong fingers of his bandaged hand pressed into her skin. Sharpness left Zane's dark eyes, and he gave her a bone-melting look. "I was going to say, he would never appreciate you. You're special, Jess. You always have been."

Because she was Janie's sister.

Zane held dear her sister's memory, closing his heart around it and not allowing anyone else into his life. He was a sought-after hunky bachelor, but he'd been true to Janie's love even now, years later. Jessica understood she was only here because Zane was too nice a guy to refuse her mama a favor. "Thank you."

He nodded and released her to go lean against the railing.

Free of his touch, she marched the glasses into the kitchen, handing them to Mrs. Lopez one at a time. She had to do something to quell her pounding heart. What the heck was wrong with her?

"*Dios*, you do not do the work around here. That's my job, no?"

"Yes. But I like to help."

It was the same conversation she'd had with Mrs. Lopez since she'd arrived here. Jessica saw nothing wrong with putting clothes in the washer and turning the thing on, or clearing the dishes, or helping slice potatoes for a meal. Today, especially, she needed to do something with her hands.

"*Sí*, okay." A relenting sigh echoed in the kitchen.

She picked up dirty dishes on the counter, loaded them in the dishwasher and put things back in the refrigerator. A few chores later, after scanning the clean kitchen they'd both worked on, she gave Mrs. Lopez a bright smile. The woman was shaking her head, but with a twinkle in her eyes. Progress.

Jessica strode out the kitchen door and was immediately knocked against the doorjamb. Pain shot to her shoulder. The jarring bump brought Mariah's face into view. "Oh, sorry."

Mariah was equally shocked from the collision. "I didn't see you."

"My fault. I should learn how to slow down."

She chuckled. "I'm the same way. I've got to get where I'm going fast, no matter if it's just to sip coffee and read the newspaper." Mariah, always impeccably dressed, rubbed her shoulder through her cognac-colored silk blouse. "Guess we're alike in that regard. Where were you going in such a hurry?"

"Nowhere. Just outside. I left Zane hanging and I wanted to go back to talk to him."

"Good luck with that. I just left him, and he's a bear right now."

"Oh, really? Why?" It couldn't be the Dylan McKay thing, could it?

"I don't know exactly what set him off other than he hates being confined. He feels like a caged animal. Though he doesn't make an effort to go anywhere, other than for business."

"I can see how that would make him restless."

Mariah smiled. "That's the perfect way to describe it. He's restless. But I'm afraid that came on well before his fall. I think a change of pace is good for him. I've helped him make the decision to open this second restaurant, and now he's thinking about movie roles. It might be just what he needs."

Or maybe he was running away from his past, the same way she was. Zane loved music. He loved writing lyrics and composing songs. He was meant to entertain. His sexy, deep baritone voice made his fans swoon. That's the only Zane she'd known.

"Dylan invited you in to hear his pitch, I understand. What did you think of the movie?"

"Me? Well, I, uh…to be honest, I think the idea of Zane and Dylan being estranged brothers coming home after the death of their father might work. If Zane can act, he'd be great in the role. The only issue I see is the love triangle about the girl back home. I saw Zane's reaction to Dylan's description of the romantic scenes he'd have to do. Zane instantly shut down. I'm not sure if Zane's up to that."

"That's exactly what I think, too. Zane's not going to do something he's not comfortable with. Believe me, I know. I've had plenty of discussions with him about his recent decisions. He bounces things off me. He asks me a question, and I tell him the truth."

"Which is?"

"I will say this. Zane can act. He's been doing so for over two years now. His public persona is far different than the real Zane." Mariah was ready to say more and then clamped shut. Her eyes downcast, she shook her head. "Forgive me. I keep forgetting who you are."

Jessica drew her brows together. "It's because of Janie. He's still hurting."

Mariah nodded. "I'm afraid so."

Mariah's eyes fell on her softly, her genuine warmth shining through. "Please forget I said anything. It's none of my business."

The idea that after two years, Zane was still making decisions based on the love he had for Janie, nestled deep into her heart. It was beautiful in a way, but also incredibly sad. "You're Zane's personal assistant. You spend a lot of time together. I can see that you care about him as a friend, too, so maybe it's more your business than mine."

"Zane thinks of you as family. He's said so a dozen times since you've come here."

"I'm the little sis he never had." Wasn't that the term he'd used this afternoon with Dylan McKay?

Stop corrupting my little sis.

Zane's loyalty to her family was very sweet. She didn't take it lightly, but she also didn't want him to think of her as a pity case. From the moment her shocked guests walked out of the church on her wedding day, weeks ago now, something harsh and cold seeped into her soul. Trust would be a long time coming, if ever again. So Zane didn't have to worry over her. She wasn't a woman looking for love. She wasn't on the rebound. He could sleep well at night.

"So, what are you up to today?" she asked Mariah. She was learning the ins and outs of Zane's superstardom. Mariah sifted through a dozen offers a day for special appearances, television interviews and charity events on Zane's behalf. She'd learned that Zane was a generous contributor to children and military charities, but lately, he'd declined any personal appearances. Mariah worked with his fan club president on occasion and took care of any personal business, such as setting up medical appointments or shopping trips. It was a different world, one that her sister, Janie, had resigned herself to because she'd been with Zane from the launch of his career. They'd grown into this life together.

"More restaurant business to do today. We've got a decorator working on the interior design, but Zane's not sure about the motif." Mariah's cell phone rang, and she excused herself.

Jessica walked over to the French door leading out to the deck. Zane was sprawled out on a lounge chair, shaded from the sun, his booted foot elevated, reading the script Dylan had brought over. Keen on the subject matter, he seemed deep in thought. As her gaze lingered, she watched him close the binder and stare out to sea, his expression incredibly wistful.

She followed the direction of his gaze and honed in on the vast view of the ocean. The sounds of the sea lulled her into a soothing state of mind. It was a place to find infinite peace, if there ever was such a thing. Her nerves no longer throbbed against her skin. These past few days, she'd been much calmer. Were time and distance all she'd needed to get over Steven Monahan? Geesh, Jessica felt at one with nature and started to believe. A chuckle rose from her throat at the notion. She was beginning to sound like a true Californian.

"Crap! Damn things."

Out of the corner of her eye, she witnessed Zane's crutches fall to the ground. The slap echoed against the wood deck. Zane was off the chair, bending to pick them up and trying to keep weight off his bad foot. It looked like a yoga move gone bad. She moved quickly, her legs eating up the length of the deck to get to him.

"Zane, hang on."

He stumbled and fell over, landing on his bad hand. "Ow!"

By the time she reached him, he was on his butt, cursing like the devil, shaking out his wrist. She kneeled beside him. "Are you okay?" she asked softly.

He tilted his head toward her. "You mean other than my pride?"

She smiled. "Yes, we'll deal with that later. How's the hand?"

"I managed to catch the fall on the tips of my fingers, so the wrist should be fine."

He moved his fingers one by one as if he was playing keys on a piano. So much for keeping his hand immobilized. "Maybe your doctor would be a better judge of that."

"Now you sound like Mariah."

"I knew an old goat like you once," she said, putting his right arm over her shoulder. "Let me help you up."

"I knew the same goat," he bounced back. "Smart critter."

"Pleeeze. Okay, are you ready? On three." She swung her arm around his waist. "One. Two. Three."

His weight drew her toward him, the side of her face against his chest, her hair brushing his shirt. He smelled like soap and lime shaving lotion. His heart pounded in her ear as she strained to help lift him.

Zane did most of the work, his brawny strength a blessing. Together, they managed to stand steady, Zane keeping weight off his foot by using her as his right crutch. Once again, just like the other night, she was wrapped tight in his arms. Ridiculous warmth flowed through her body. She couldn't explain it except she felt safe with him, which was silly because this time she'd done the rescuing. "There," she said, satisfied she'd gotten him upright. "Now, we're even."

His arm over her shoulder, he turned to her with eyes flickering. "Is that so?"

Well, maybe not. She was getting drunk on him, minus the alcohol. "Yes, that's so."

"I could've gotten up on my own, you know."

"It wouldn't have been pretty."

He laughed. "True."

"So, I'm glad I was here to help. Show a little gratitude."

He wasn't a man who liked taking help. That was part of the problem. His gaze roamed over the deck where he'd spent most of his day, and she sensed his frustration.

"Wanna get out of here?" he asked.

"Sure. Where would you like to go?" Mariah said he didn't like to go out, so she couldn't let this opportunity pass by. If he needed some breathing room, away from his gorgeous house and his familiar surroundings, who was she to deny him?

"Anywhere. I don't care. Are you up to driving my car?"

"I can manage that. I'm going to get your crutches now, okay?" She didn't wait for an answer.

She released him and he stood there, balancing himself for the two seconds it took her to pick up both of his crutches and hand them over. Tucking one under each arm, he pointed a crutch toward the door. "After you."

Three

To her surprise, Zane picked his silver convertible sports car for her to drive over the black SUV sitting in his three-car garage. The other car, a little blue sedan, had to be Mariah's car. Jessica helped him get into his seat, taking his crutches and setting them into the narrow backseat before closing his door.

As soon as she climbed behind the steering wheel, she understood why Zane didn't venture out much. Sitting in the passenger seat, he was encumbered by his foot, broken in three places, which required him to be extremely careful. He also put on a disguise. Well, a Dodgers baseball cap instead of his signature Stetson and sunglasses wasn't much of a disguise, but she knew where he was coming from. He couldn't afford to be recognized and surrounded by fans or paparazzi. In his condition, he couldn't make a fast getaway. "Why am I driving this car?"

"More fun for you."

"You mean more scary, don't you? How much is this car worth, just in case I wreck it, or—heaven forbid—put a scratch on it?"

He smiled. "Don't worry. It's insured."

Stalling for time, she fidgeted with her glasses and took several deep breaths before she turned to Zane. He was still smiling at her. At the moment, she didn't enjoy being his source of amusement.

"Here goes." With the press of a button, the engine purred to life. Zane showed her how to adjust her seat and mirrors using the control buttons. Once set, she supposed she was as ready as she would ever be. She pumped the gas pedal and gripped the steering wheel. She'd never driven anything but a sedan, a boring four-door family car with no bells and whistles. This car had it all. A thrill shimmied up her legs…all that power under her control.

She backed the car out of the garage and made the turn into a long driveway that reached the front gate. Upon Zane's voice command, the gate slid open, and she pulled forward and onto the highway. She drove along the shoreline, keeping her eyes trained on the road and her speed under thirty miles per hour.

His back was angled against the passenger door and his seat. She sensed him watching her. He'd opted to keep the top up on the convertible, for anonymity, she supposed. Even though he'd not had a hint of scandal to his name, every time Zane went out, he risked being photographed. Putting the top down on his car in the light of day would be like asking for trouble.

She didn't dare shoot him a glance, keeping her focus on the road.

"What?" she asked finally. "Your grandmother drives faster than me?"

"I didn't say a word." His Texas drawl seeped into her bones. "But now that you mention it, I think my great-grandmother drove her horse and buggy a mite faster than you."

"Ha. Ha. Very funny. Maybe I'd drive faster if I knew where I was going."

He sighed. "I've learned that sometimes, it's better not to know where you're going. Sometimes, planning isn't all it's cracked up to be. Some roads are better not mapped out."

After that cryptic statement, she did look his way and found him resting his head against the window. His sunglasses hid his eyes and his true expression. The mood in the car grew heavy, and she didn't know how to answer him, so she buttoned her lips and continued to drive.

After five minutes of silence, Zane shifted in his seat. "Wanna see the site of the restaurant? The framework is up."

"I'd love to."

He directed her down a side road that wound around a cove. Then the beach opened up again to a street that faced the ocean. Unique shops and a few other small restaurants sparsely dotted the shoreline before she came upon the skeletal frame of a building.

"There it is. You can park along the side of the road here." He gestured to a space, and she swung the car into the spot.

"This is a great location."

"I think so, too. On a clear day, there's visibility for miles going in either direction."

The beach was wide where the restaurant would sit, far enough from the water to avoid high tides. A rock embankment jutted out to the left, where pelicans rested, scoping out their next meal. Above them and across the road, far up on the cliffs sat zillion-dollar homes overlooking the coastline.

"Do you want to get out?" she asked.

"Yep."

"Hold on," she said, killing the engine and climbing out. She reached into the backseat and grabbed his crutches, then strolled to his side of the car. He was lifting himself out of his seat by the time she got there. "Here you go."

"Thanks."

She waited for him to get his bearings, and they moved through the sand until they reached the beach side of the restaurant. "So this is Zane's on the Beach."

"Yep. Gonna be."

"I suppose it's good that you're branching out. You've become a regular entrepreneur."

"Can't sing forever."

Why not? Willie Nelson, George Strait and Dolly Parton weren't having career problems. And neither was Zane. "Why do I get the feeling you're not eager to go back to doing what you love to do?"

It was a personal question. Maybe too personal, given that Zane didn't react to it at all. He simply stared at the ocean, thinking.

"I'm sorry. It's none of my business."

"Don't apologize, Jess," he rasped with a note of irritation. "You can ask me anything you want."

Okay, she'd take him up on that. "So, then, why are you searching for something else when you've established yourself as a superstar and you have fans all over the world waiting for your return?"

He closed his eyes briefly. "I don't know. Maybe I'm tired of being in my own skin."

It was the most honest answer he could've given her. Zane was hurting. Still. And he didn't know how to deal with it. "I get that. After my disastrous breakup with Steven, I felt totally out of options. I didn't know who to trust, what to believe. I couldn't make a decision to save my life. That's why when I had to get out of Dodge, I let my mother take over and make arrangements. After she did, I didn't have the gumption to argue with her. No offense, but visiting you wasn't even on my radar."

He chuckled. "Should I be insulted?"

She softened her voice. "You made a point of keeping away from the entire family after Janie…"

He winced at her honesty. Maybe she shouldn't have been so blunt. "It's not for the reasons you think."

"I know why you did it, Zane."

He put his head down. "I was having a hard time."

"I know." He'd been swallowed up with guilt. Janie was five months pregnant when she lost her life. Zane was touring in London, and Janie wanted desperately to travel with him. Zane had given her a flat-out no. He didn't want her away from her doctors, on a whirlwind schedule that would sap her energy. They'd argued until Zane had gotten his way. He'd loved Janie so much, trying to protect her and keep her safe. It was a tragic irony that she'd died in her own home on the night Zane had performed for Prince Charles and the royal family. Momentary grief swept over his features. He'd probably feel the guilt of his decision until his dying day. But there was no one to blame. No one could've known that Janie would've been safer in London than resting in her own sprawling, comfortable ranch house while Zane was gone. Her mother had recognized that. Jessica recognized that, but Zane wouldn't let himself off the hook.

Braced by the crutches under his arms, Zane let go of one handle and took her right hand. Lacing their fingers, he applied slight pressure there, squeezing her hand as they stared at the ocean. "I'm glad you're here, Jess."

Peace and pain mingled together, a bittersweet and odd combination of emotions that she was certain Zane was experiencing, too. They'd both lost so much and shared a profound connection.

Afternoon winds blew her hair onto her cheek and Zane touched her face, removing the wayward strands, tucking them behind her ear. "It's good to have someone who understands," he whispered.

She nodded.

"You can trust me," he said.

"I do." Strangely, she did trust Zane. He wasn't a threat to her, not the way every other man in the universe might be. She had learned some harsh lessons about men and about herself. She'd never overlook the obvious the way she had with Steven. She'd never allow herself to be fooled into believing a relationship would work when there were three strikes against it from the get-go.

"This is nice," she murmured.

"Mmm," he replied.

Zane released her hand, and they fell into comfortable silence, watching wave upon wave hit the shore. After a minute, he turned her way. "Do you want to see the inside of the restaurant?"

Her gaze was drawn to the framed, unroofed, sandy-floored structure behind her. "I sure do!"

He laughed. "Follow me, if you can keep up." He hobbled ahead of her. "I'll give you the grand tour."

Zane folded his arms and leaned back in the booth of Amigos del Sol—friends of the sun—watching Jess pore over the menu items of his favorite off-the-beaten-path Mexican restaurant. It was a small hacienda-style place known for making the most delicious, fresh guacamole right at the table. "Everything is great here, but the tamales are out of this world."

And the guacamole was on its way.

Jessica's head was down, and her glasses dropped to the tip of her nose. With her index finger, she pushed them up to the bridge of her nose. He grinned. It was a habit of hers that he found adorable.

"Tamales it is. I will bow to your vast culinary taste. But I'm even more impressed at how you managed to sneak us in the back way and get this corner booth."

"I shouldn't give away my secrets, but while you were navigating turns and learning how to gun the engine on my car, I texted Mariah to call the owner and let him know we needed a quiet spot and we'd appreciate coming in through the back door."

"Ah…Mariah. Your secret weapon."

"She makes things happen."

"I've noticed. She anticipates your every move and watches out for you."

"Yeah, like a mother hen," he said. "Not that I'm ungrateful. She's like my second right arm." He lifted his broken wrist. "And in my condition, that's important."

A uniformed waiter pushed a food cart to their table. Zane practically salivated. He'd been craving the home-made guacamole since earlier in the day. The waiter set out a *molcajete* and *tejolote*, a mortar and pestle carved from volcanic rock, to begin preparations. Squeezing lime juice into the bowl first, he added cilantro, bits of tomato, garlic and other spices. Next he used the pestle to grind all the flavors together and scooped out three perfectly ripe avocados. The aroma of the blended spices and avocados flavored the air. Once done, the guacamole and warm tortilla chips were placed on the table.

After the waiter took their dinner order, he walked off with his cart. Zane grabbed a tortilla chip and dipped it into the fresh green mixture, offering it to Jess first. "Taste this and tell me it's not heaven."

She leaned in close enough for him to place the chip into her mouth. As she chewed, a beautiful smile emerged, and her eyes closed. She sighed. "Oh, this is so good."

Drawn to the sublime expression on her face, he forgot about his craving for a few seconds. Eyeing her reaction distracted him in ways that might've been worrisome, if it hadn't been Jess. As soon as she finished chewing, she snapped her eyes open. "You didn't have one yet?"

"No…it was too much fun watching you."

"I seem to be a source of your amusement lately."

That much was true. Jess being here brightened up his solemn mood. That wasn't a bad thing, was it? He dipped a chip in and came up with a large chunk of guacamole. He shoved it into his mouth and chewed. On a swallow, he said. "Oh, man. That's good."

Jess's eyes darted past him, focusing on something happening behind his back.

"Uh…oh. Don't turn around, Zane," she whispered.

As soon as her words were out, two twentysomething girls approached the table, giddy and bumping shoulders with each other. "Hello. Excuse me," one of them said. "But we're big fans of yours."

"Thank you," he said.

"Would you mind signing a napkin for us?"

He glanced at Jessica and she nodded.

"Sure will."

They produced two white napkins and a pen, which made things a little less awkward. Zane hated waiting around while fans scrambled for something for him to autograph. They gave him their names, and he signed the napkins and handed them back.

"Thank you. Thank you. You're our favorite country singer. I just can't believe we've met you. Your last ballad was amazing. You have the best voice. I saw you in concert five years ago, when I was living in Abilene with my folks."

Zane kept a smile on his face. The girls were clueless that they were interrupting his meal with Jessica. "Well, that's nice to hear."

They stared at him, hovering close.

Jessica stood up then. Bracing her hands on the table, she smiled at the girls. "Hello. I'm Jessica, Zane's sister-in-law." The girls seemed baffled when she shook both of their hands. "We were having a little family talk, and we're limited on time. Otherwise I'm sure Zane would love to speak to you. If you give me your names and addresses, I'll see that you get a signed CD of his latest album. And please be discreet when you leave here," she whispered. "Zane loves meeting his fans, but we really need a few private moments during our meal tonight."

"Oh, okay. Sure," one of them said congenially.

The other girl wrote their addresses on the napkin Jessica provided before she wished them well. Giggling quietly, the two women walked away.

Zane stared at Jessica. "I'm impressed."

"I've been listening to how Mariah deals with your fan club members. I hope it's okay that I offered them a CD."

"It's fine. Happens all the time. I wish I'd have thought of it myself."

"They were persistent."

Zane shook his head. "I could tell you stories." But he wouldn't. Some of the things that had happened to him while touring on the road weren't worth repeating. "Actually, these two were a little subtle compared with some of the people who approach me."

"You mean, compared with the *women* who approach you."

He scrubbed his chin, his fingers brushing over prickly stubble. "I suppose."

Jessica snorted. "You don't have to be modest on my account. I know you're in demand."

He tossed his head back and laughed. "In demand? What are you getting at?"

"You're single, available, successful and handsome. Those two women who left here would probably describe you as a hottie, a hunk, a heartthrob and a hero. You're in the 4-H club of men."

His smile broadened. "The 4-H club of men? You just made that up."

"Maybe," she said, taking a big scoop of guacamole and downing the chip in one big swallow. "Maybe not."

"You constantly surprise me," he said, sipping water. He could use something stronger. "I like that about you."

"And I like that you're decent to folks who admire you."

Their eyes met, and something warm zipped through his gut. Jessica's compliments meant more to him than ten thousand wide-eyed, giddy fans. He admired her, too. "Ah, shucks, ma'am. Now you're gonna make me blush."

Another unladylike snort escaped through her mouth. Zane grinned and leaned way back in his seat just as his cell phone rang. Dang, he didn't want to speak to anyone now, but only a few close friends and family knew his number. He fished the phone out of his pocket. "It's Mariah," he said to Jessica. He turned his wrist to glance at his watch. It was after eight. "That's odd. She usually texts me if she needs me for something after hours. Excuse me a second."

"Hi," he said. "What's up?"

"Zane, s-something terrible's h-happened." Sobs came through the phone, Mariah's voice frantic and unsteady. Zane froze, those words instilling fear and flashing a bad memory. "My mother had a stroke. It's pretty b-bad."

"Oh, man. Sorry to hear that, Mariah."

"I have to fly home right away. Th-they don't know... oh, Zane...she's so young. Only sixty-four. She never had health problems before. Oh, God."

"Mariah, you just do what you have to do. Don't worry about a thing." Her voice broke down, her sobs growing louder. "Where are you?"

"At Patty's h-house in Santa Monica." She shared a place temporarily with an old college roommate. The situation was perfect while he was staying on Moonlight Beach. She was close by without living under his roof.

"Pack up a few things and try to stay calm. Do you have a flight?"

"Patty got me on a midnight flight to Miami."

"Okay...I'll send a car for you in an hour. Hang in there, Mariah."

"It's okay, Zane. I a-appreciate it, but Patty offered to d-drive me. I'll be fine." A deep, sorrowful sigh whispered through the phone. "Are you going to be all right? I don't know how long I'll be gone."

"Don't worry about me." He stared at Jessica. Her eyes were softly sympathetic and kind. "Take all the time you need. And call if there's any way I can help, okay?"

"Okay. Thanks. Goodbye, Zane."

Zane hung up the phone. "Man, that's rough. Mariah's mother had a stroke. She's on her way to Florida now."

"Gosh, I'm sorry to hear that. Is it serious?"

"Seems that way." He ran a hand down his face, pulling the skin taut. "I've never heard her so unraveled before. She may be gone a long time."

"I would think so. Will you find a replacement for her?"

Zane wasn't thinking along those lines. Not yet. He kept hearing the disbelief and pain in Mariah's voice and understood it all too well.

Your wife didn't make it, Zane.

Didn't make what? he'd asked the doctor over and over, screaming into the phone. Then, all the way home from London, he kept thinking, hoping, praying it had been a mistake. A horrible, sick mistake. It wasn't until he saw the desolate ruins of his once proud home in Beckon that it finally sank in Janie was gone. Forever.

The meal was served, and as his gaze landed on the plate of saucy cheese-topped tamales, blood drained from his face, and his gut rebelled. For Jessica's sake, he pushed his haunting memories aside. He didn't want to ruin her meal.

Jessica reached for him across the table, her fingertips feathering over his good hand gently, comforting him with the slightest touch. When he lifted his lids, he gazed into her knowing, sensitive eyes, and she smiled. "Let's have them pack up this food. We'll eat it later on."

"Do you mind?" he asked.

"Not at all. I'm ready to go anytime you are."

He felt at peace suddenly, a glowing warmth usurping the dread inside his gut.

And then it hit him. Sweet Jess. She was good for him. She understood him, perhaps better than anyone else on this earth. She was a true friend, an authentic reminder of home, and he needed her here.

"You asked me before if I'd find a replacement for Mariah."

"Yes, I did. Hard shoes to fill, I would imagine."

"Yeah, I agree." He looked her squarely in the eyes. "Except I've already found someone, and I'm looking straight at her."

Four

Jessica woke to a glorious sunrise, the stream of light cutting through early morning haze and clouds in a host of color. Every morning brought something new from the view outside her bedroom window, and she was beginning to enjoy the variance from fog to haze to brilliance that took place before her eyes.

She stretched her arms above her head, working out the kinks, not so much in her shoulders and neck, but the ones baffling her brain. Last night, Zane told her to keep an open mind and sleep on his suggestion of replacing Mariah as his personal assistant. Her mouth had dropped open, and she thought him insane for a few seconds, but then he pointed out that he wasn't working, he had no gigs lined up, and he wasn't doing interviews right now. Most of what she had to do was hold off the press and postpone anything pending to future dates.

She wouldn't go into it cold. Mariah would be in touch to give her the guidance she needed to get her through anything remotely difficult.

"You're an intelligent woman, Jess. I'm convinced you'd have no problem, and I'm right here to help you," he'd said.

Zane's assurances last night gave her the push over the edge she'd needed this morning. Her head was clear now, and she valued the challenge and even looked forward to it. She wasn't ready to return to Texas anyway. Zane wanted freedom from his agent and manager's constant urging to get back on the horse. Zane wasn't ready yet and she could understand that. He needed more time, just as she did.

The new, bronzer Jessica no longer had freckles on her nose, thanks to a wonderful suntan that had connected those freckly dots and browned up her light skin. How many more hours could she feasibly sunbathe her day away? Staying on for a few weeks and helping Zane out would give her a new sense of purpose.

Jessica showered and dressed quickly. Putting on a pair of khaki shorts and a loose mocha-brown blouse, she slipped her feet into flip-flops and strode toward the kitchen. There were no wickedly delicious aromas drifting from the kitchen this morning. Mrs. Lopez had yet to arrive.

"Sonofabitch!"

A string of Zane's profanities carried to her ears. She grinned. Poor guy. He hated being confined.

She ventured into his bedroom. "Zane?"

"In here!"

She followed the sound of his cursing. He was standing over the bathroom sink, and their eyes met in the mirror. A scowl marred his handsome face, and three blood dots covered with bits of tissue spotted his cheeks and chin. Remnants of lime-scented shaving cream covered the rest of his face. "Damn hand. It's impossible to get a good shave."

"Whoops." With her index finger, she caught a drop of blood dripping from his chin before it landed on his white ribbed tank. "Got it."

He peered at her in the mirror and handed her a tissue. "Thanks."

"Thank me later, after I shave you. We'll see if I can't do a better job."

"You?"

"I used to lather up my dad and shave him when I was a kid." She hoisted herself up onto the marble counter to face him and picked up his razor. "It used to be a game, but darn it, I did an excellent job. Dad was surprised. Seems I'm pretty good with one of these."

Doubtful eyes peered at the razor in her hand.

"What? You don't trust me? It's a guarantee I'd do a better job than what I see on your face now. Or, I can drive you to the local barbershop. Since I'm going to be your new personal assistant and all."

The scowl left his face immediately, and her heart warmed at seeing approval in his eyes. "You've decided, then?"

"Yes, I'm on the clock now. So what will it be? A shave by your PA or a drive to the barber?"

"Try not to cut me," he said.

"You've already done a good job of that." She handed him a towel. "Wipe your face clean. We'll start from scratch."

Zane's eyes widened.

She chuckled at her bad choice of words. "You know what I mean." Pressing down on the canister, she released a mound of shave cream in her hand and leaned forward to rub it over his cheeks, chin and throat.

Zane leaned a little closer, his body braced by the counter. Her heart did a little dance in her chest. His nearness, the refreshing heady lime scent, her position sitting on the counter, *touching him*—suddenly she was all too aware of the intimate act she was performing on her brother-in-law.

What on earth was she doing?

Zane needed help and she'd rushed to his aid. But she hadn't thought this through.

He still towered over her, but only by a few inches now. She lifted her eyes and found him, waiting and watching her through the mirror.

Her hand wasn't so steady anymore.

She couldn't fall down on her first official act as Zane's personal assistant, intimate as it was.

"Okay, are you ready?"

He kept perfectly still. "Hmm."

Her legs were near his hip, and she angled her body to get closer to his face. Bracing her left hand on his shoulder to steady herself, she was taken by the strong rock-hard feel of him under her fingertips. She stroked his face, and the razor met with stubble and gently scraped it away. Carefully she proceeded, gliding the razor over his skin in the smoothest strokes she could manage.

His breath drifted her way as heat from his body radiated out, surrounding her. Cocooned in Zane's warmth, she fought an unwelcome attraction to him by thinking of Steven, the man who'd shattered her faith. And that reminder worked. Thoughts of Steven could destroy any thrilling moment in her life. She dipped the razor into the sink and shook it off. Zane's gaze left the mirror, and as she lifted her eyes to his, there in that moment, a sudden surprising sizzle passed between them.

One, two, three seconds went by.

And then he focused his attention back on the mirror, keeping a silent vigil on her reflection.

"How are you holding up?" she asked, breaking the quiet tension.

"Am I bleeding?"

Her lips hitched at his intense tone. "No."

"Then, I'm good."

Yes. Yes, he was.

"Okay, now for your throat. Chin up, please."

He obeyed without quarrel. Gosh, he really did trust her. Something warm slid into her belly, and the feeling clung to her as she finished up his shave.

"All done," she said after another minute. "Not a nick on you, I might add." At least one of them had come out of this unscathed.

"I think I hear Mrs. Lopez tinkering in the kitchen now." She handed him his razor and jumped down from the counter. "Do you want breakfast? Coffee?"

She was partway out the door when Zane caught her arm

just above the elbow. He looked gorgeous in his white ribbed tank, his face and throat shaved clean but for the last traces of shave cream. "Just a sec. I haven't thanked you. And you don't have to worry about breakfast for me."

"I don't?"

"No. That's not part of your job description."

Well, duh. She knew that. Mariah hadn't served him his meals, but Jessica couldn't very well tell him she'd run her mouth in order to get away from him as quickly as possible.

"We'll go over what I expect of you as my assistant this morning. Thanks for the shave." He slid his hands down his smooth face, and his eyes filled with admiration. "Feels great. You're pretty good."

She swallowed. Did this mean she'd have to shave him every day?

Gosh, she really didn't think this through thoroughly enough.

"Thanks. Well, I'll see you at breakfast."

"Oh, and Jess?"

"Yeah?"

He released her arm. "I'm glad you'll be staying on. I do need your help. And I think you'll enjoy it, but whenever you're ready to head home, I'll...understand."

"Thanks, Zane. I'll do my best."

Four hours later, Jessica sat behind the desk in Zane's office, satisfied she had things under control. It had been a little scary at first. What did she really know about Zane's celebrity life? But Mariah had been acutely efficient, keeping good records and documenting things, which made it easier for Jess to slide into the role of personal assistant. She seemed to live by a detailed calendar, and Zane's appointments, events and meetings were clearly labeled. *Thank you, Mariah, for not being a slouch.* In the day planner she came to regard as The Book, Mariah had jotted down phone numbers next to names and brief reminders of what needed to be said or done.

No to the *People* magazine interview.

Yes to donating twenty thousand dollars to the Children's Hospital charity. Zane would make an appearance in the future.

No to an appearance on *The Ellen DeGeneres Show*.

And so on.

With a little help from Zane earlier this morning, she was able to field a few phone calls and make the necessary arrangements for him. It was clear Zane was in a state of celebrity hibernation. Other than opening a new restaurant, Zane was pretty much in a deep freeze. Maybe he needed the break away from the limelight, or maybe he wasn't through running away from his demons.

In a sense, she was doing the same thing by being here, afraid to go home, afraid to face the pitfalls in her own life. She, too, was hiding out, so she had no right to judge him or try to fix the situation. It wasn't any of her business. That was for sure.

"How're you doing?" he asked.

She glanced up from The Book to find him standing at the office threshold, leaning on his crutches. She flashed back to shaving him this morning and the baffling emotions that followed her into breakfast. Her heart tumbled a little.

"Good, I think."

He smiled. "Anything I can help you with?"

"No, not at the moment."

He didn't leave. He didn't enter the room.

"Is there anything I can do for you?" she asked.

"Sort of." His lips twisted back and forth. "You see, Dylan's bugging me about this script. Fact is, I don't know if acting is right for me. I never had an acting lesson in my life. So I want to say no to him. But…"

She braced her elbows on the desk and leaned forward. "But, just maybe it's something you want to do?"

He stared at her. "Hell, I don't know, Jess. I guess I need a reason to say no."

"And how can I help you with that?"

"Dylan's got this idea that if I had someone run lines with me, I'd feel better about accepting the role. Or not. I didn't ask Mariah, well…because she works for me and I'm not sure she would be—"

"Honest?"

"Objective. She tends to encourage me to try new things, so she might not be the person to ask."

"So you're saying I'd have no problem telling you 'you suck'?"

He chuckled. "Would you?"

"No, no problem at all."

His brows gathered. "I'm not sure how to take that."

"I'd have only your best interests at heart. But honestly, Zane, what do I know about acting? What if my instincts aren't dead-on? What if I get it wrong?"

"Bad acting is bad acting. You can tell if someone sings off-key, can't you?"

"Sometimes, but my ear for music isn't as good as yours."

"But you're *real*, Jess. You would know when something is authentic. That's all I'm asking you to do."

His faith in her was a heady thing. She couldn't deny she was flattered. And as his personal assistant, she couldn't really tell him she didn't want to do it.

"Okay. What did you have in mind?"

"We read through some scenes. See if I can grasp the character."

"Where?"

He pointed to the long beige leather sofa—the most comfortable place to sleep in Zane's world. "Right here." He hobbled into the room on his crutches and sank down, resting the crutches on the floor. "The script is behind you on the bookcase. If you could get it and bring it over…"

"Sure." She turned and found it quickly. *"Wildflower?"*

"That's the one. You know most of the story."

She did. She was there when Dylan explained the premise of the romantic mystery to both of them the other day. It was about a man who comes home to his family's ranch after a long estrangement and finds his brother romantically involved with the woman he'd left behind. There's a mystery surrounding their father's death and a whole cast of characters who are implicated, including both brothers. "I think it's a good story, Zane."

"Well, let's see if I can do it justice."

"Sure."

She walked over to the couch and took a seat one cushion away from him.

"I don't think that's going to work," Zane said. "You have to sit next to me." He waved the script in the air. "There's only one of these."

"Right." As she scooted closer to him, Zane's eyes flicked over her legs and lingered for half a second. Oh, boy. The back of her neck prickled with heat. In a subtle move, she adjusted her position and lowered the shorts riding up her legs to midthigh. Zane didn't seem to notice. He'd focused back on the script and was busy flipping through story pages.

"Okay, here's a scene we can do together. It's where Josh and Bridget meet for the first time since his return."

She peered at the pages and read the lines silently. It was easy enough to follow. There were one or two sentences of description to set up the scene and action taking place. The rest was dialogue, and each character's part was designated by a name printed in bold letters.

"You start first," he said, pointing to the top of the page. "Where Josh speaks to Bridget in front of her house."

"Okay, here goes." She glanced at him and smiled.

He didn't smile back. He was taking this very seriously. She cleared her throat and concentrated on the lines before her. "Josh? You're home? When did you get back? I…I didn't know you'd come."

"My father is dead. You thought I wouldn't return for his burial?"

"No. I mean…it's just that you've been gone so long."

"So you wrote me off?"

A note of anger came through in Zane's voice. It was perfect.

"That's not how it happened. You left me, remember? You said you couldn't take living here anymore."

"I gave you a choice, Bridget. You didn't choose me."

"That wasn't a choice. You asked me to leave everything behind. My family, my friends, my job and a town I love. I don't hate the way you do."

"You think I hate this place?"

"Don't you?"

"Once, I loved everything about this place. Including you."

Jessica stared at him. The way he dropped his voice to a gravelly tone and spoke his lines was so real, so genuine, it impressed the hell out of her.

"But you've moved on." Now Zane's voice turned cold. He had a definite knack for dialogue. "With my brother."

They read the next three pages, bantering back and forth, learning the characters and living them. The scene was intense, and Zane held his own. He had a lot of angst inside him and found his release using the screenwriter's words on the page.

The scene was almost finished. Just a few more lines to go.

"Don't come back here, Josh," she said, meeting Zane's eyes. "I don't want to see you again."

Zane was really into the character now. "That's too bad, Bridget." The depth of his emotion had her believing. "I'm back to stay."

"I'm going to marry your brother."

"Like hell you are," Zane said fiercely, leaning toward Jessica, his face inches from hers.

"Don't…Josh…don't mess with my life again."

"This is where he grabs her and kisses her," Zane whispered. His breath swept over her mouth, and she found herself wanting to be kissed. By Zane. Heat crept up her throat and burned her cheeks.

Zane glanced at her mouth. Was he thinking the same thing? Did he want to kiss her?

He was a man she trusted. He was a man she truly liked. "Do you want to, uh, bypass the kiss?"

He shook his head, his gaze dropping to her mouth. "No," he rasped. "I don't."

Her pulse pounded as he took her head in his hands and caressed the sides of her overheated cheeks with his long, slender fingers. Her head was tilted slightly to the left, and then his mouth lowered to hers. He touched her lips gently, and she felt the beautiful connection from the depths of her soul. Was she supposed to stay in character? How would she accomplish that? Everything inside her was spinning like crazy.

The script called for a brutal, crushing kiss, but this kiss was nothing like that. His lips were firm and giving and generous…pure heaven.

"I'm not through messing with your life, Bridget." The gravel in his voice convinced her. He did *harsh* perfectly. "I might never be through."

As Zane backed away, his gaze remained on her. He blinked a few times, as if coming to his senses, and then cleared his throat.

The air sizzled around her. Was Zane feeling it, too? She didn't know where to look, what to say.

"It's your line," Zane whispered.

Oh! She glanced at the page and read her last line. "I—I can't do this again, Josh."

Zane paused for a second, glaring at her for a beat. "I'm not gonna give you a choice this time."

There. They'd made it through the entire scene. Zane flipped the script closed, and as he braced his elbows on his knees, he leaned forward.

Her heart was zipping along. She needed space, a few inches of separation from Zane. She flopped back against the sofa and silently sighed.

"Thank you," Zane said quietly.

"Hmm."

"Now for the hard part. I respect your opinion. No hard feelings either way, so lay it on me."

He'd convinced her he could act. Aside from the kiss that still had her reeling, she was completely enthralled with his character. He'd stepped into Josh's shoes without a bit of awkwardness. "I'm no expert, but I know when something's good. I'd say you were a natural, Zane."

He leaned back and looked into her eyes. Oh, God. She didn't want him to notice how nervous she was. "You really think so?"

"I do. You dove into that character and had me believing."

He stroked his jaw and sighed.

"I'm sorry if you wanted to hear you stink at acting. But I don't think so."

A crooked smile lifted the corner of his mouth. "I admit, I was hoping that was the case. Makes my decision harder now."

"Sorry?" she squeaked.

He released a noisy breath. "Don't be. I asked for your opinion. I appreciate you, Jess," he said. "I trust your judgment. I, uh…sort of got caught up in the scene. Hope you didn't mind about the little kiss I gave you."

Little kiss? If that was his little kiss, what would a real, genuine, from-the-heart kiss feel like from her one time brother-in-law? He didn't know the kiss had sent her senses soaring, and it would have to stay that way.

She'd never admit she'd wanted to kiss him. He was her brother-in-law, for heaven's sake. He was her employer now. And he was a good, decent man who'd never take advantage of her situation. She knew all that about Zane.

Of course he'd wanted to stay true to the script. He'd delved so deeply into character that he didn't want to lose the momentum of the scene. But, oh…for that brief moment when he'd looked into her eyes and her heartbeat soared, she believed he, Zane Williams, really wanted to kiss her.

And it had been a wow moment. "No, I didn't mind at all."

Her cell phone on the desk rang and she jumped up to answer it. "Oh, uh, excuse me, Zane. It's Mama."

"Sure."

He began to rise, and she put up her hand. She wasn't going to have him leave his own office. "No, don't get up. I'll take it in my room." Her mother's timing couldn't have been better. She needed to get away from Zane and the silly notions entering her head.

She walked out of the office and climbed the stairs. "Hi, Mama."

"Hi, honey. How're you doing this afternoon? Oh, I guess it's still morning there."

"Yes, it's just before noon. I'm doing fine." Her heartbeat had finally slinked down to normal since Zane's kiss a few minutes ago.

"Really?"

"Yes, I'm fine." It was weird how distance and the new surroundings made her see things differently. She wasn't thrilled with the way her life was turning out—she'd invested a lot of time on Steven Monahan—but she didn't need to worry her mother over it. Right now, she was taking it one day at a time. "Actually, I'm glad you called this morning. I have news. Zane's personal assistant, Mariah, had to take a leave of absence. Her mother's very ill and, well, since I'm here and Zane needs help, he's asked me to take over the position. It's temporary, but I won't be coming home this week or the next, probably. I might be here longer than that."

"Oh, that's good, honey."

"It is?" There was something in her mother's too-cheerful tone that raised her suspicions. She entered her bedroom wondering what was up? "What I mean to say is, I'm sorry Mariah's mother is ill. Bless her heart. I'll be sure to say a prayer for her. But you staying there for a little longer might be best for you, after all."

Really? Her overprotective mother—the woman who had set her alarm at 3 a.m. every night to get up and check on her two sleeping little girls when they were young, the woman who'd worried and fretted during their teen years, and the woman who, after Jessica's disastrous nonwedding, arranged for her to move into Zane's house just so he could keep an eye on her—*that mother* was actually glad that she wasn't coming home anytime soon?

Now she knew something was going on.

She lowered herself onto the bed. "Why, Mom? What's happened?"

"I hate to tell you this, honey. But better it come from me than you hear about it another way."

Her heart nearly stopped. Was her mother ill? Was it something severe? She flashed back to Janie's death. How the news had seemed unreal. She'd gotten physically sick, acid drenching her stomach and her breaths coming in short, uneven bursts. Now she held her breath. "Please, just tell me."

"Okay, honey. I'm sorry…but I just found out that your Steven eloped with Judy McGinnis. They just up and left town two nights ago. Went to Vegas, I hear. The whole town's crackling about it."

"W-with Judy?"

"I'm afraid so. I never expected that from Judy. Honey, are you okay?"

She might never be okay again. She'd just learned that the man she'd banked on for three full years, the man who had sworn up and down in her dressing room on their wedding day that he wasn't ready for marriage and that it wasn't anything she'd done, had just gotten married. The fault was all his for not recognizing his problem sooner, he'd told her. She'd believed he had commitment issues. But now she knew the truth. He wasn't ready for marriage to *her.* Instead, he chose one of her bridesmaids to speak vows with.

Judy had been her friend since grade school. Oh, God. She'd accepted losing Steven and any future they might've had together, but losing Judy's friendship, too? That was a double blow to her self-esteem. They'd both betrayed her. Made a fool out of her. She hadn't seen the signs. How long had Judy and Steven been hooking up behind her back?

Her eyes burned with unshed tears.

Being here and having a new sense of purpose in helping Zane, she was beginning to feel better and gain control of her emotions. But now, fresh new pain seared her from the inside out. What an idiot she'd been. That was the worst part of all, this hopeless sense of loss of *herself.* Her heart ached in a way it never had before. She felt herself slipping away.

She couldn't give in to it. If she did, she'd be totally lost. She couldn't dwell. She wouldn't let their betrayal dictate her life. She wouldn't curl into a pitiful ball and let the world spin without her.

"Jessica?"

"I'm going to be fine, Mama. I just need some time to digest this."

"I'm here if you need me, honey. I'm so, so sorry."

"I know. I love you. I'll call you tonight. Bye for now."

Jessica pushed End on her cell phone and faced the mirror. Her mousy-brown-haired reflection stared back at her through tortoiseshell-rimmed glasses. "What's happened to you, Jess?" she muttered.

She was tired of feeling like crap. Being a victim didn't suit her. She wasn't going to put up with it another second. The old Jessica had to go.

It was time for her to take hold of her life.

Afternoon breezes whispered through Zane's hair as he sat on his deck, gazing out to sea. Dylan McKay sat beside him, sipping a glass of iced tea. He didn't mind Dylan's company as long as he wasn't pressuring him about taking on an acting role.

"How soon before you're all healed up and ready to start living again?" Dylan asked.

Not soon enough for him. The confinement was getting to him. The only good thing about being temporarily disabled was that he didn't have to make any decisions right away. And he was milking that for all it was worth.

"The blasted boot comes off on Monday."

"And how's the wrist doing?"

His wrist? He flashed to trying to shave himself this morning. He'd been hopeless. Mariah usually took him to the barber twice a week. He hated being so damn helpless, and Jess had rescued him. She'd given him a clean, smooth shave and for a second there, as she leaned in close to him, her honeyed breath mingled with his and his body zinged to life. Electricity stifled his breathing for those few moments.

Jess?

He'd written it off as nothing and gone about his business.

Then he'd asked Jess to read lines with him. He'd gotten so caught up in the scene that when it came time to kiss her…he didn't want to deny himself the opportunity. Had it been only because the scene demanded a kiss? Or had it been something more?

A tick worked his jaw. It damn well couldn't be something more.

Though kissing her soft giving mouth packed a wallop. He'd forgotten what it felt like to have a sweet woman respond to him. He'd backed off immediately and didn't dare take it any further. The complication was the last thing either of them needed.

"My wrist should be healed soon, too…with any luck." He wiggled the tips of his fingers unencumbered by the cast. "I can't do a damn thing left-handed. You have no idea how uncoordinated you really are until you lose the use of your right hand."

"I hear you. How long will Mariah be gone?"

"Not sure. I spoke with her this morning. Her mom might have some permanent paralysis. Mariah's pretty torn up about it."

"So it's just you and Jessica now, living in this itty-bitty ole house?"

Zane rolled his eyes. The house was enormous, much more than he needed. He was hardly bumping into her in the hallway in the middle of the night.

Now, there was a thought. He struck that from his mind.

"She's taken on Mariah's duties here."

"You hired her?"

Zane nodded. Dylan didn't need to know that having Jessica around made him feel closer to Janie. She, above everyone else, understood the loss he felt. They shared that horrific pain together. Jess was *home* to him, without him having to return to Beckon. He liked that about her. So maybe it was selfish of him to ask her to stay on, but he hadn't pressured her. Much. He'd like to think she wanted to stay.

"I did. I didn't have a backup for Mariah. You know as well as I do it's hard to find a replacement for a trusted employee. I trust Jess. She'll do her best."

Dylan eyed him carefully. "You sure sing her praises."

"She's bright and learns quickly." He shrugged. "She's family."

"You keep saying that."

"It's true. Why wouldn't I say it?"

Dylan flashed a wry smile and then shook his head. "No real reason, I guess. Any chance I can convince you to be my costar before you head back on tour?"

"I haven't made up my mind yet, McKay. I told you I'm not making you any promises."

"Yeah, yeah. So I've heard. Remember what they say about people who drag their feet."

"No, what the hell do they say?"

"They risk getting them cut off at the ankles."

He laughed. "I should be flattered you're so persistent. Honestly, if I lose the role to someone else, so be it. I'm not sure." About anything, he wanted to add.

"Buddy, you're not going to lose the role to someone else. I'm the executive producer, and I see you doing this character."

"You want my fan base."

"That, too. I'd be a fool not to want to reel in your fans. I know they'd turn out for you. But I have no doubt in my mind you'd be—"

"Zane?" A sultry voice carried to the deck. His heart stopped for a second. Sometimes, when he was least expecting it, Jess would call out his name and he'd swear it was Janie asking for him.

"Out here," he called to her.

Jessica popped her head out the doorway. "Oh, sorry. I didn't realize you had a guest."

"Hi," Dylan said. "How're you doing, Jess?" Dylan sent her a brilliant smile. The guy could charm a billy goat out of a field of alfalfa.

"Hi, Dylan."

"Come on out here, Jess." Zane hadn't seen much of her since they'd run lines and *kissed* earlier in the day. He'd heard her working in the office, but she hadn't asked for his help, and he'd let her be. "Have a cool drink with us?"

"Uh, no thanks," she said, taking a few steps toward them. She wore a loose-fitting flowery sundress. Her hair was up in a ponytail, and a straw satchel hung from her shoulder. "Actually, I finished up what I could this afternoon. I was hoping to go shopping now. I wanted to see if you needed anything while I was out."

"Oh, yeah? What are you shopping for?" Was he so dang bored that he had to nose into Jessica's private business?

"I, uh, didn't bring enough clothes with me. I thought I'd pick up a few things."

"Hey, I know a great little boutique in the canyon," Dylan said. "I'd be happy to drive you there."

Zane swiveled his head toward Dylan. Was he kidding?

Jessica chuckled. "Thanks, that's a kind offer, but I'm good. I'm anxious to explore and see what I can find."

"Gotcha," Dylan said. "A little me time. I hope Zane hasn't been working you too hard."

"Not at all. I'm enjoying the work." With her finger, she pushed her sunglasses up her nose. She did that when she was nervous, and obviously, Dylan McKay made her nervous. Zane wasn't sure that was a good thing. He inhaled deep into his chest. Jessica was vulnerable right now, and she didn't need Dylan hitting on her.

"But you're both coming to the party tomorrow night, right?" Another charming smile creased his neighbor's face.

"Nope, sorry," Zane said. "We're not available."

Jessica faced him a second and blinked, then shifted her focus to Dylan. "Actually, I've changed my mind. I'd love to come. What time?"

Dylan's grin seemed to spread wider than the ocean view. "Six o'clock."

"I'll be there."

"You will?" Zane asked. They'd both decided on not going.

She nodded. "Sure, why not? Sounds like fun."

Zane couldn't argue the point. If she wanted to go to Dylan's little party, he had no right to stop her. "Well, then... I guess we're coming."

"We?" Jessica asked. A genuine spark of delight lit her expression. "You're going now? That's great, Zane."

He shrugged it off but couldn't stop his chest from puffing out. Why did it make him so doggone happy that Jessica wanted him around?

"Well, I'd better be off. Zane, is it still okay that I take one of your cars?"

"Yep. You know where the keys are in the office."

"Okay, thanks. I'll take the SUV. Bye for now," she said. She pivoted and walked back into the house.

"She's nice," Dylan said.

"Very nice. "

"Too nice for me? Are you warning me off?"

"Damn straight I am." Zane eyed him. "You know darn well Jessica isn't your type. So stay away. I'm serious. She's had it rough lately."

The patio chair creaked as Dylan leaned over the arm and focused on him. "You like her?"

"Of course I like her. She's like my..." But this time Zane couldn't finish his thought. He couldn't say she was like a sister to him. An image of taking her mouth in a daring kiss burst through his mind again. In that moment, he'd forgotten she was Janie's sister. All that filled his mind was how sweet and soft her lips were. How much he wanted to go on kissing her. He'd felt at peace with Jess, yet electrified at the same time.

He'd had women in the past to satisfy his physical needs. He hadn't been a total saint after Janie died, but he hadn't had a real relationship, either, and he sure as hell wasn't going in headfirst with Jessica. So why in hell was the memory of kissing her earlier torturing him?

"I meant you want her for yourself."

Zane snorted. "Are you not hearing what I'm saying? She's off-limits. To everyone. She has a lot of healing to do. Until then, no one gets near her." He'd promised her mother he'd protect her and make sure she didn't get hurt again.

"Okay, okay. I get it, Papa Bear. Now, let's get back to the script. I think Josh's character is perfect for you, like it was written with you in mind."

For once, Zane was grateful the subject changed to his possible acting career.

Five

Thank goodness for credit cards. They gave Jessica the freedom to spend, spend, spend at the boutique Mariah had once raved about. She scoured the golden wardrobe racks at Misty Blue, and every time something struck her as daring and unlike her small-town schoolmarm image, she handed it to Misty Blue's *attire concierge* to put aside for her to try on. Sybil, the thirtysomething saleswoman, was dogging her, making suggestions and flattering her at every turn.

"Oh, you must have that," and "you'll never find a better fit," and "you'll be the envy of every woman on Moonlight Beach," were her mantras.

Jessica ate up her compliments. Why not? She needed them as much as she needed to buy a whole new wardrobe. The old Jessica was put to rest the minute she'd heard about her so-called good friend eloping with her fiancé. So be it. Jessica would return to Beckon a new woman.

Her clothes would be stylish. Her attitude would brook no pity. And she'd have a few thousand dollars less in her very tidy bankroll.

Saving money wasn't everything.

"I'll just put these items in your dressing room," Sybil announced. "Take your time looking around. When you're ready, you'll be in the Waves room."

Jessica blinked. Even the dressing rooms had names. "Okay, thank you."

She moved around the boutique slowly, taking her time perusing the shelves and racks. She picked out a two-piece bathing suit, a few hip-hugging dresses, two pairs of designer slim-cut jeans, and four blouses in varying colors and styles.

Sybil came racing forward. "Let me take those off your hands, too. I'll put them in the dressing room."

She transferred the clothes into Sybil's outstretched arms. "Thanks."

"Would you like to keep shopping?"

Jessica eyed several pairs of shoes on top of a lovely glass display case. "Yes, I'll need some shoes, too."

"I'll have Carmine, our shoe attendant, help you with that."

Thirty minutes later, Jessica glanced around the Waves dressing room. Clothes hung on every pretty golden hook, and shoes dotted the floor around her feet. She'd gone a bit hog-wild in her choices and needed guidance from someone who knew her well. She punched the speed dial on her cell phone and was relieved when her best friend, Sally, answered.

"Help me, Sally. I need your honest opinion," she whispered. "I texted you pictures of five of the dresses I've tried on. Did you get them?"

"Sure did. I'm looking at them now."

"Good." The inventor of cell phone technology was a genius. It made shopping a whole lot easier. "Which ones do you like?"

"Gosh, none of them look bad on you. You have a great figure," Sally said, almost in disbelief. "You've been hiding it."

"I guess I have." She'd never been comfortable with her busty appearance and had always chosen clothes to hide rather than highlight her figure. Now, all bets were off.

"Did you like the red one?"

"Definitely the red. That's a given," Sally said. "Whose eyeballs are you trying to ruin?"

"What do you mean?"

"That dress is an eye-popper."

She pictured Zane. Why had he come to mind so easily? It was ridiculous and yet, something had hummed in her heart when he'd kissed her today. He'd been caught up in the scene. She shouldn't make a darn thing out of it. But she was having a hard time forgetting the feel of his lips claiming hers. As short as the kiss was, it had been potent enough to shoot endorphins through her body. That wasn't necessarily a good thing.

"Do you think maybe I shouldn't be doing this?" she asked Sally, her bravado fading.

"Doing what? Pampering yourself? Spending some of your hard-earned money on yourself? Indulging a little? I'm only sorry I'm not there to help you with your TLC gone wild. Believe me, if I could swing it, I'd hop on a plane today."

She chuckled. "TLC gone wild? That's a new one, Sal."

"I'm clever. What can I say? Buy the clothes, Jess. I'll let you decide on the shoes, but those red stiletto heels will kick some major butt. Oh, and while you're at it, lose the eyeglasses. You brought your contacts, didn't you?"

"Yes, I have them."

"Well, use them. If you're going to do it, do it right."

Of course, Sally was dead-on. If she was going to invest in these clothes, she had to go all the way. She'd already decided to ditch her tortoiseshell glasses. Her hair could use some highlights, and her California tan was coming along nicely. Already she felt better about herself.

"And Sal, I wish you could come out here. It's really… nice."

"I bet. Zane's place sounds like heaven. Right on the beach. I bet you don't even have any swamp heat and humidity."

"Nope, not like home."

"Tell me you haven't met any big movie stars and I swear I won't be jealous."

"I, uh, well," her voice squeaked.

"Who? Tell me or I'll haunt you into forever."

"Would you believe Dylan McKay lives two doors down?" Jessica squeezed her eyes shut, anticipating the bombardment. No one was a bigger fan of the Hollywood heartthrob than her bestie Sally.

"You've met him?"

"Yes, I sort of ran into him on the beach." Or rather, the other way around—he'd run into her. "He's a friend of Zane's."

"No way! I can't believe it. Tell me everything."

A knock on the dressing-room door startled her, and she jumped. She'd forgotten where she was.

"Miss Holcomb, can I help you with anything?" Sybil asked.

"Whoops, gotta go," she said in a low voice. "I've got to get dressed. I'll call you later."

"You better!"

Jessica smiled as she ended the call and answered the saleswoman. "No thanks. I'm doing great.

"I'll be out in one minute."

"You sound happy. Find anything to your liking?"

"Just about everything," she answered.

She imagined the attire concierge who worked on commission smiling on the other side of the door.

Her purchases today would make both of them happy.

Zane had received a text message from Jessica half an hour ago telling him not to wait for her to have his meal. She was going to be late. But he didn't feel much like eating without her. It had taken Jessica living here for him to realize he'd eaten too many meals alone.

She must've gotten carried away on her little shopping spree.

When Jessica finally pulled through the gates, driving toward the garage, Zane made his way to the living room and, with the grace of an ox, plunked down onto the sofa.

A minute later the door opened into the back foyer, and he heard the crunch of bags and footsteps approaching. He picked up a magazine and flipped through the pages.

"Hi, Zane," Jessica said. Her voice sounded breezy and carefree. "Sorry I'm so late."

When he lifted his head, he found her loaded down with shopping bags. "Did you buy out the store?"

She chuckled from a warm and deep place in her throat. "Let's just say the store manager couldn't do enough for me. They offered me a vanilla latte and a chocolate mini croissant, and the shoe salesman almost gave me a foot massage."

His brows gathered. "A foot massage?"

"I told him no. I didn't have time. Is that done here?"

"I don't know if it's done *anywhere*," Zane said. For heaven's sake, she was buying shoes, not asking for a damn foot rub. His nerves started to sizzle. He studied the assortment of shiny teal-blue bags she held. "Where did you go?"

"Misty Blue. Mariah recommended the shop to me. It's just up the coast."

"Leave it to Mariah," Zane muttered. She had impeccable taste, but she could be indulgent at times.

"Speaking of Mariah, have you heard from her today?"

"Yes, we spoke earlier this morning. Do you need to talk to her about anything in particular?"

She shook her head and lowered her packages to the floor, releasing the handles. "I'm managing for right now." She walked over to lean her elbows on the back of his angular sofa. From his spot on the couch, he had a clear view of her face. "How is her mother doing?"

Zane shook his head. "Not great." He was lucky his mother and father were in their seventies and still quite active living in a retirement community in Arizona. He saw them several times a year. And when something like this happened, he thought about spending more time with them. "Mariah said her mom might have some permanent damage from the stroke, but it's too soon to tell. She spends most of her day at the hospital or meeting with doctors."

"I'm sorry to hear that."

"Yeah, me, too. And with all that, she asked about you. She made me promise to have you call her with any questions."

Jessica sent him a rigid look. "Unless it's an emergency, I'm not going to call her, Zane. You and I both know what it's like having to deal with a family crisis."

A lump formed in his throat. "Yeah. I agree, and I told her as much. There's nothing so important that it can't wait. Between the two of us, we'll figure out what needs figuring from this end."

"Right. Hey, I almost forgot. I bought you a present."

His heavy heart lightened. "You did?"

She bent to forage in one of the bags and came up holding a long, shiny black box. It wasn't a gift from Misty Blue, that was for sure. She stretched as far as her arms could reach, eyeing the box carefully one last time, before handing it over. "I, uh, hope this doesn't upset you, but I know how much you loved the one Janie got you, and, well…this one is from me."

Her fingers gently brushed over his hand, and her caring touch seized his heart for a moment. With his good hand, he managed to lift the lid and gaze at his gift. He found himself momentarily speechless. It was an almost identical replica of a bolo tie with a turquoise stone set on a stamped silver backing that Janie had given him on the anniversary of their first date. It had been lost in the fire, and he'd never replaced it. It wouldn't have had the same sentimental meaning. But the fact that Jessica gave it to him meant something. He lifted the rope tie out of the box and shifted his gaze to her. "It's a thoughtful gift, Jess."

"I know you treasured the first one. I helped Janie pick it out, so I remember exactly what it looked like."

"You didn't have to do this." But he was glad she had.

"You're putting a roof over my head and feeding me, but more importantly, being here is helping me heal. It's the least I could do for you. And I wanted it to be…something special."

"It is. Very special."

He rose from the sofa, found his footing and, using his crutches, shuffled over to her. He gazed through the lenses of her glasses to dewy, softly speckled green eyes. They were warm and friendly and genuine. He bent to kiss her forehead the way a brother would a sister, but then aware-ness flickered in her eyes, and he felt it, too. He lowered his mouth, heady in his need to taste the giving warmth of her lips again. When he touched his mouth to hers, he sa-vored her sweetness and assigned this moment to memory for safekeeping. He backed away just in time to keep the kiss to one of thanks. "Thank you."

"You're welcome." Her deep, sultry voice thrilled him and churned his stomach at the same time. She sounded so much like Janie.

"I haven't had dinner yet. I waited for you. Mrs. Lopez put our meal in the oven to keep warm. Are you hungry?"

"Starving," she said. "Shopping is tough. I worked up an appetite."

He laughed. The women he knew loved to shop and spend endlessly. He'd never heard one remark about hard work.

"I'll put the bags away in my room. Meet you in the kitchen?"

He nodded. He hated that he couldn't offer to help her. He watched her climb the stairway holding three maxed-out shopping bags in one hand and two in the other. The next time she wanted to shop, he'd be damn ready to take the packages off her hands and carry them upstairs for her.

Zane made his way into the kitchen. Mrs. Lopez had left chicken and dumplings warming in the oven. Zane lifted a periwinkle-striped kitchen towel tucked over a basket and eyed cheesy biscuits, still warm. He dipped into the basket and sank his teeth into a biscuit. Warmth spread throughout his mouth and reminded him he was ready for a hearty meal.

"Wow, smells good in here." Jessica entered the kitchen.

"Mrs. Lopez made one of my favorites tonight."

"In that case, I'm surprised you waited for me."

"I figured a Southern girl like you would appreciate sharing chicken and dumplings. It's my mother's recipe."

"You figured right. Well, then. Have a seat." She gestured to the table. "I'll dish it up. Unless you want to eat outside?"

He shook his head. The sun had already set, and winds howled over the shoreline, spraying sand everywhere. "Here is just fine."

Before he knew it, the table was set, plates were dished up and he had the company of one of his favorite people sitting across from him.

The chicken was tender, the dumplings melted in his mouth and Zane spent the next few minutes quietly diving into his meal. He liked that he could sit in silence with Jess without feeling as though he had to entertain her. She was as comfortable with the quiet as he was.

"Mmm, this was so good." Jess took a last bite of food, and as she wiped her mouth, his gaze drifted down to where the napkin touched her lips. "I'll have to steal the recipe from Mrs. Lopez and make it for my mother when I get home."

"No problem." He shouldn't be noticing the things he was noticing about Jess. Like the cute way she pushed her glasses up her nose, or the way she smelled right after a shower, or how her light skin had burnished to a golden tone from days of sunbathing. The sound of her voice dug deep into his gut. Janie and Jess were the only two women he knew that had a low, raspy yet very feminine voice. Janie had been sultry, sexy, alluring, but…Jess?

"Zane?"

He lifted his gaze to her meadow-green eyes.

"You went someplace just now."

"I'm sorry."

"No need to be sorry. Are you okay?"

He nodded and cleared his throat. "So, did you have fun shopping today?"

"Fun?" Her head tilted as a slow, easy smile spread across her face. "I had an attire concierge help me. That was weirdly entertaining. She dogged my every step but was nice as can be. Actually my best friend, Sally, helped me make the right choices. Sally was my maid of honor in the wedding that never was."

"Is your friend in town?"

She laughed and shook her head. "No, not at all. I texted her pictures of the clothes I tried on, and she helped me decide. I'm *so* not a shopper."

"Ah, the power of technology."

"Yeah, ain't it great?"

It beat having Dylan McKay help her shop. Zane wasn't about to allow that to happen.

A heartbreaking ladies' man was the last thing sweet Jess needed in her life right now.

"Actually, it is pretty great. I'm glad you had a good day."

"I plan to have a lot of good days from now on." A glint of something resolute beamed in her eyes, her face an open expression of hope.

Jess was healing, and that was a good thing. He liked seeing her feeling better. That was the whole point of her coming here. But it seemed too soon. And she seemed a little too happy for a woman who'd been betrayed and heartbroken. Right now, Jessica Holcomb looked ready to conquer the world, or at least Moonlight Beach. Instincts that rarely failed him told him something else was going on with Jess.

And he didn't know if he was going to like it.

"Hi, Zane." Jessica stepped into the living room, dressed and ready for Dylan's party.

Zane turned from the window… His hair was combed back, shiny and straight, the stubble on his face a reflection of not having a shave in two days. He looked gorgeous in a white billowy shirt and light khaki trousers. When his gaze fell on the *new* her, his lips parted and his eyes popped as he took in her appearance from the top of her head to her sandaled toes. Pain entered his eyes, and he blinked several times as if trying to make it go away. Relying on the two crutches under his arms, he straightened to his full height and sighed heavily.

"Zane?" Her lips began to quiver. What was wrong with him? "Are you all right?"

He stared at her, his expression unreadable. "I'm fine."

"Are you? Have I done something? Don't you like the dress?" Her mind rushed back to the clothes she'd laid out on the bed. She'd chosen the cornflower-blue sundress that accented her slender waist in a scoop-neck design that, granted, revealed more cleavage that she was comfortable with, but wasn't indecent by any means.

His mouth opened partly, but no words tumbled forth, and then he gulped as if swallowing his words.

"What is it?" she pressed.

"You look like Janie," he rushed out, as though once pressured, he couldn't stop himself from saying it.

"I…do?"

How could she possibly look like Janie? Janie was stunning. She had natural beauty, a perfectly symmetrical face. She wore stylish clothes, had the prettiest long, silken hair, and oh…now she understood. Of course she and Janie resembled each other—they were sisters—but Jessica had always stood in Janie's shadow where beauty was concerned. Her blonde-from-a-bottle hair color had turned out a little less dark honey and much more sweet wheat, similar to Janie's hair color. Jessica didn't usually wear her contacts, but she imagined her eyes looked more vibrant green than ever before. Like Janie's brilliant gemstone eyes. Did Zane think he was seeing a ghost of his former wife? She didn't believe she looked enough like Janie for that and never thought about how it might appear. "I, um, wasn't trying to, but I take that as a compliment." She shrugged, compelled to explain. "I guess I needed a change."

An awkward moment passed between them, which was weird. They didn't do awkward. Usually they were completely at peace with each other.

"You didn't need to change a thing," he said firmly.

Was he trying to make her feel better? Even she had to admit, after looking at herself in the mirror today, that her new look made her appear revitalized and well, better than she had in years. Zane had no idea what she was really going through right now, the pain, rejection, anger. He didn't know, because she hadn't told him. He wasn't her shrink, her sounding board. And call it pride, but she wasn't ready to talk about Steven's quick marriage to her once-friend/bridesmaid to anyone, much less him. "I'm sorry if I upset you. Obviously you don't approve. I don't have to go tonight."

The last thing she wanted to do was cause Zane any upheaval in his life. He was still in love with Janie. She got that. No one knew what a special person her sister was better than she did.

She was staying here thanks to Zane's generosity. He was her employer now, too, and she had to remember that, yet underlying hurt simmered inside her. He had no idea how hard this was for her. She'd come into this room hoping for some sort of approval. She'd made a change in her appearance, but it was more than that. She looked upon this makeover as a fresh start, a way to say "screw you" to all the Stevens in the world. She'd come into this room with newfound confidence, and Zane's dismal attitude had caused her heart to plummet. Why did it matter so much to her what Zane thought?

She pivoted on her heels, taking a step toward the staircase, and Zane's voice boomed across the room. "Damn it, Jess. Don't leave."

She whirled around and stared at him. A dark storm raged in his eyes.

Was he angry with her? Maybe she should be angry with him. Maybe she'd had enough of men dictating what they wanted from her. "Is that an order from the boss?"

"Hell, no." His head thumped against the window behind him once, twice, and then he lowered his voice. "It wasn't an order."

"Then what was it?"

Zane's gaze scoured over her body again, and as he took in her appearance, approval, desire and *heat* entered his eyes. Her bones could have just about melted from that look. Then, with a quick shake of his head, he said, "Nothing, I guess. Jess, you don't need my approval for anything. Fact is, you look beautiful tonight. You surprised me and, well…I don't like surprises."

She didn't move. She was torn with indecision.

From the depth of his eyes, his sincerity came through. "I'm a jerk."

Her lips almost lifted. She fought it tooth and nail, but Zane could be charming when he had to be.

"Blond hair looks great on you."

She drew breath into her lungs.

"The dress is killer. You're a real knockout in it."

His compliments went straight to her head. He'd finally gotten to her. "Okay, Zane. Enough said." She'd been touchy with him, maybe because she'd hoped to impress him a little. Maybe because, in the back of her mind, she'd wanted to please Zane or at least win his approval. "Let's forget about this." She didn't like confrontation, not one bit.

"You'll go to the party?"

She nodded. "Yes. I'm ready."

They'd had their first real argument. Granted, it wasn't much of one. A few minutes of tension was all. But she'd stood her ground, and she could feel good about that. One thing that loving Steven had taught her was never to turn a blind eye. From now on, she wanted to deal in absolute truth.

"You mind driving?" he asked.

"I should make you trudge through the sand all the way to Dylan's place."

"I'd do it if it would put a smile back on your face."

"It's tempting. But I'm not that cruel."

Amused, Zane's mouth lifted, and they seemed back on even footing again.

Whatever that was.

Six

Zane stood outside in the shadows, his shoulder braced against the wall of Dylan's home. The setting sun cast pastel colors across the cobalt sky, and waves pounded the shoreline. The Pacific breezes had died down and no longer lifted Jessica's blond locks into a flowing silky sheet in the wind. She stood in front of a circular fire pit on the deck. Her flowery summer dress had been a victim of the wind, too, and hell if he hadn't noticed her hem billow up, *every single time*. And every single time, something powerful zinged inside him.

He couldn't figure why Jessica had made such a drastic turnabout in her appearance. He wouldn't have called her an ugly duckling before—she'd been perfect in her own natural way—but tonight, she'd bloomed into a beautiful swan and he feared he was in deep trouble.

He liked her. A lot. And he knew damn well she was as off-limits to him as any woman would ever be. The old Jess he could deal with. She was like his kid sister. But now, as he watched the predusk light filter through her hair and heard the sound of her sultry laughter carry to him as she spoke with Dylan and his friends, she seemed like a different woman.

Sweet Jess was a knockout, and every man here had noticed.

Dylan popped his head up from the group and gestured to him. "Come on over and join the party."

Well, damn. He couldn't very well stay in the shadows the entire night. He'd have to shelve his confused thoughts about Jessica and join them. He pushed off from the wall using his crutches for balance and made his way over to the fire pit.

"I thought Adam was the only recluse on the beach," Dylan said.

"There's a difference between savoring one's privacy as opposed to hiding out from the world," Adam said.

Adam Chase was his next-door neighbor, the architect of many of the homes on the beachfront and a man who didn't give much away about himself. He'd been featured in *Architectural Digest* and agreed to a rare magazine interview, but mostly the man's astonishing work spoke for itself. The one thing he'd learned about Adam in the time he'd known him was that he shied away from attention.

"He's got you there, Dylan. Being someone who craves attention, you wouldn't understand." Zane zinged him because he knew Dylan was a good sport and could handle the teasing.

Dylan took Jess's hand, entwining their fingers. "They're ganging up on me, Jess. I need someone in my corner."

Jess's giggles swept over Zane, and he eyed the half-empty blended mojito she held in her other hand. She freed her hand and inched away from Dylan. It was hardly a noticeable move, except maybe to Zane, who was eyeballing her every step. "You boys are on your own. I'm staying out of this."

Dylan slammed his hand to his chest. "Oh, you're breaking my heart, Jess."

Adam's eyes flickered over Jess and touched on the valley between her breasts in the revealing sundress she wore. She was dazzling tonight, and Zane had a hard time keeping his eyes off her, too. He shouldn't fault the guys for flirting, yet every inappropriate glance at her boiled his blood.

"You're a smart woman, Jessica," Adam said.

"The smartest," Zane added. "She's going home with me tonight."

All eyes turned his way. Ah, hell. He'd shocked them, but no more than he'd shocked himself. He spared Dylan a glance, and the guy's smug grin was bright enough to light the night sky. Adam's face was unreadable, and the four others around the fire pit became awkwardly silent. "She's my houseguest and she's…"

"I think what Zane meant," Jess chimed in, "was that I've had a tough time lately. I'm getting over a broken engagement and, well, he's sweet enough to want to protect me." Her eyes scanned the seven people sitting around the fire pit. "Not that I'd need protecting from anyone here. You've all been so nice and welcoming."

They had. And now Zane felt like an ass for staking his claim when he had no right and for putting her in an awkward position.

"But I do make my own decisions. And I'd love to get to know each of you better."

"You *are* a smart woman." Dylan turned to Zane with genuine understanding. He and Dylan had had this conversation before. "And we all knew what Zane was getting at."

Zane clamped his mouth shut for the moment. He'd said enough, and he had a feeling that Jessica wasn't too thrilled with him right now. His big brother act had probably started to wear thin on her. He didn't say boo when she walked down to the water deep in conversation with Adam Chase for a few minutes. He didn't register an inkling of irritation when Dylan offered to give her a tour of his house. But darn if he wasn't keenly relieved when Jessica made friends with three of the women at the party. She'd spent a good deal of time with them. He recognized one woman as an actress recently cast in a film about a Southern girl. She'd gobbled up a good deal of time asking Jess questions about Texas.

"You look like you could use a beer." Adam handed him one of the two longnecks he clasped between his fingers.

"You read my mind. That sounds good." Adam's mouth twitched. The man didn't often smile, but obviously Zane had amused him. "Right. How's the restaurant coming?"

Zane had asked Adam for a recommendation of someone whose specialty was designing shoreline commercial establishments since Adam didn't work with small restaurants. "We've broken ground. The framework is up, and we should open our doors in a few months. I'm hoping for Labor Day."

"Glad things are going smoothly."

He nodded. Last year, he'd opened a restaurant in Reno, and his friend and CEO of Sentinel Construction had overseen the building. But Casey's business didn't reach the west coast, and Adam had connections all over the world. He wound up hiring a builder Adam said was top-notch. "They seem to be."

Adam sipped his beer. "Jessica seems like a nice girl. She said she's indirectly related to you."

Indirectly? Though those were true words, it still stung hearing them coming from her mouth secondhand that way. There was something painful in the truth, and if he was being gut-honest with himself, it was liberating, as well. "Uh, yeah. She was my wife's little sis. She's staying in Moonlight Beach for a while."

"With you. Yes, you made that clear earlier." Adam's mouth hitched again. It was more animation than Zane had seen in the guy practically since he'd met him. "I'm going out on a limb here, but either you're hooked on her, or you've got a bad case of Big Brother syndrome."

Zane peered over Adam's shoulder and caught a glimpse of Jessica speaking with a man who looked enough like Dylan to be his twin. "Who the hell is that?"

Adam swiveled his head and gave the guy a once-over.

"Dylan introduced him to me before you arrived. That's Roy. He's Dylan's stunt double."

Roy and Jessica stood in the sand under the light of a tiki torch and away from the crowd of people beginning to swarm the barbecue pit, where a chef prepared food on the grill. Zane didn't like it, but he couldn't very well pull her away from every guy who approached her.

"So, which is it?" Adam asked.

"Which is what?" He watched Jessica laugh at something Roy said.

"Are you playing big brother? Cause if you're not, I think you have to amp up your game, neighbor. Or you're going to lose something special, before you know what hit you."

Zane stared at Adam. The guy had no clue what he was talking about. Adam had no idea how hard he'd loved Janie. He had no idea how he couldn't get past what happened. He'd tried over and over to put his emotions to lyrics, to gain some sort of closure in a song meant to honor his love for Janie, but the words wouldn't come. "I've already lost—"

Adam began shaking his head. "I'm not talking about the past, Zane. I'm talking about the future."

"Spoken by a man who rarely steps foot out of his house."

Now Adam did laugh. "I'm here now, aren't I?"

"Yeah, that surprises me. Why are you?"

He shrugged. "I've got a temperamental artist painting a wall in my gallery. It's going to be fantastic when he's through, and he insists on complete privacy. I'm staying at Dylan's for a few days."

"Well, damn. You're sorta here by default, then."

"It's not so bad. At least I got to meet Jessica and all her Southern charm."

"Why, that's very nice of you to say, Adam."

A sweet strawberry scent wafted to his nostrils, announcing Jessica's presence even before she'd uttered a word.

He'd come to recognize her scent, and every time she approached, a little bitty buzz would rush through his belly. She took a place by his side, and he refrained from puffing out his chest.

"Just speaking the truth," Adam said.

"Hey, Jess," Zane said.

"Hey, yourself," she said to him. He wasn't sure if she'd been deliberately avoiding him since his dopey remark earlier, or if she was flitting around like a butterfly to make new friends. Either way, he was glad she'd come over to him.

"Having fun?"

"Sure am. I'm meeting some great people here. It was sweet of Dylan to invite me. Sorry if I abandoned you."

He raised his beer bottle to his lips. "No problem. I spent my time keeping Adam amused."

Jessica shot a questioning glance at Adam.

"He's quite a party animal these days," Adam explained, tucking his free hand into his trouser pockets.

Zane gulped the rest of his beer. He wouldn't be here if Jessica hadn't changed her mind about coming. "C'mon Jess. Looks like the meal's being served. I've got me a hankering for some barbecue chicken."

"Adam, will you join us?" she asked.

Adam shook his head. "I'll see you over at the table later. I'm going to have another drink first."

Zane began moving, and Jessica kept by his side as he headed for a table occupying the far corner of the massive patio. "Chances are we won't see much of Adam tonight. He keeps to himself pretty much."

"Does he?" she asked. "Why?"

"I don't really know. We got friendly when I leased the house from him. And we had some business dealings, but I sensed he's a loner. It's probably why he was standing with me, over against the wall."

"Well, he was cordial to me."

"Yeah, I know." Zane dipped his gaze to the swell of her breasts teasing the top of her frilly sundress. Her skin looked creamy soft and—Lord help him—inviting. With that blond hair flowing down her back and her eyes as green as a grassy meadow, she made his heart ache. "I saw the two of you walking out to the water."

"All I did was ask him about his designs. Architecture has always fascinated me."

"Yeah, that's probably why he spent time with you. He loves talking shop." Lucky for him, Jess didn't notice the sarcasm in his voice. He managed to pull a chair out for her, crutches and all.

Man, he'd be glad to rid himself of them.

It couldn't happen soon enough.

They'd stayed at the party a little too long. Zane was smashed, going over his liquor limit an hour ago, and now she struggled to get him out of the car. He obviously didn't take his own advice. Hadn't he warned her of not drinking too much, because in his handicapped state, he wouldn't be able to help her? Well…now the shoe was on the other foot. "Hang on to me," she said, reaching inside the car.

"Glad to, darlin'."

He slung his arm around her shoulder, nearly pulling her onto his lap.

"Zane!"

An earthy laugh rumbled from his throat.

"Not cute."

"Neither are y-you," he said.

After a few seconds of maneuvering, she managed to get him upright.

"You're b-beautiful."

Oh, boy. She rolled her eyes and ignored his comment.

He swayed to the left. Sure-footed he was not. She leaned him up against the car. "Here." She shoved a crutch under his arm, tucking it carefully but none too gently. "Please, please, try to concentrate."

Maybe she should've taken Dylan up on his offer to drive Zane home. But Zane wouldn't have any of it, insisting he could manage.

Men and their egos.

Now she had two hundred pounds of sheer brawn and muscle to contend with. "Lean against me, Zane. Try not to topple. Ready?"

He nodded forcefully, and his whole body coasted away from her. "Whoa!" She gripped him around the waist and tugged with all of her might to bring him close. Letting him go right now would be a disaster. "Don't make sudden moves like that."

"Mmm."

He sounded happy about something. She was glad someone was enjoying this. When he seemed secure in his stance, she took a step and then another. With his body pressed to hers and one shoulder supporting his arm, she managed to get him through the garage and inside the house. By the time she made it to his bed, her strength was almost sapped. "Here we go. I'm going to let go of you now."

"Don't," he said.

"Why? Are you feeling dizzy?"

He shook his head, and his arm tightened around her shoulder. She was trapped in his warmth, his heat. And as she gazed up into his eyes, they cleared. Just like that. The haze that seemed to keep him in a woozy state was gone. "No. I'm feeling pretty damn good. Because you're here with me. Because I can't get you out of my head."

As if his own weight was too much to bear, he sat down, taking her with him. She plopped on the bed, and the mattress sighed. Streaming moonlight filtered into the room, and their reflection in the window bounced back at her. Two souls, searching for something that they'd lost. Was that what the attraction was?

"Are you drunk?" she asked.

"Not too much anymore." He pushed aside her hair at her nape, his touch as gentle as a Texas breeze. He nipped her there, his teeth scraping around to the top of her throat and the sensation claimed all the breath in her lungs.

"You sobered up fast," she whispered, barely able to form a coherent thought. Having his delicious mouth taking liberties on her neck was pure heaven.

"I know when I want something."

His nips were heady, and she tilted her head to the side, offering him more of her throat. "Wh-what do you want?"

With his good hand under her chin, he turned her head, and then his lips were on hers, pressing firm against her softness, igniting fireworks that started with her brain and rushed all the way down to her belly. She turned to him, roping her arm around his neck, kissing him back. He smelled like pure male animal, his scent mingling with whiskey and heat. Her breasts perked up, and her nipples pebbled against the silky material of her dress.

"I want to kiss you again and again," he rasped over her lips. "I want to touch your body and have you touch mine. I need you, too. So badly, sweetheart."

Oh, wow. Oh, wow. Oh, wow. A fierce physical attraction pulled at her like a giant magnet. She couldn't fight the force or the combustible chemistry between them. And Zane didn't give her time to refuse. With his left hand, he began unbuttoning his shirt and did a lousy job of slipping the buttons free until she came to his rescue.

"Let me." She shoved his hand away and quickly finished for him. With his shirt open now, his chest was a work of art, muscled and bronzed. She itched to touch him, to put her hands exactly where he wanted her to. She inhaled, and as she released a breath, she spread her palms over his hot, moist skin. From the contours of his waist up his torso to where crisp chest hairs tickled the underside of her fingers, she savored each inch of him.

A guttural groan exploded in the room, and she wasn't sure if she'd made that sound, but one look into Zane's eyes darkened by desire and she knew it wasn't her.

He was on fire. His skin sizzled hot and steamy, his breathing hitched and all of that combined was enough to blanket her body with burning heat. "We can't," she said softly.

She had to say it. Because of Janie. Because of Steven. She and Zane were both trying to heal, but none of that resonated right now. None of it seemed powerful enough to derail the sensations whipping them into a frenzied state.

Maybe this was what both of them needed.

One night.

His mouth claimed her again as he lay down on the bed, tugging her along with him. She fell beside him. Promptly he snaked his arm under her waist and flipped her on top of him.

She had his answer. Yes, they could.

His good hand cupped her cheek, and his eyes bored into her. "Don't question this, Jess. Not if it's what you want right now."

That was Zane. The man who didn't plan for the future anymore, the man who'd said it was better sometimes not to know where you were going. And Jessica certainly didn't have a clue what her future held or where the heck she was going from here.

But she knew what she wanted tonight.

How could she not? Her breasts were crushed against Zane's chest, her body trembling and so ready for whatever would come next. Zane was a good, decent man who also happened to be sexy as sin but he had also been her sis— She stopped thinking. Enough. She might talk herself out of this. "It's what I want."

He gave her a serious smile and kissed her again, his lips soft and tender, taking his time with her, making her come apart in small doses.

In the moment, Jessica gave herself permission to let go completely. He pushed the straps down on her dress and her breasts popped free of restraint. Zane caressed her, running his hand over her sensitive skin, lightly touching one wanton crest that seemed made for his touch.

A deep moan rose from her throat. She closed her eyes and enjoyed every second of his tender ministrations. "You have a beautiful body, sweetheart," he said, then rose up to place his mouth over one breast, his tongue flicking the nub, wetting it in a flurry of sweeps. He moved to the other side and did the same, a little more frenzied, faster, rougher. She squealed, the exquisite pain sending shock waves down past her belly.

Zane reacted with a jerk of his hips. "Get naked for me, Jess."

She pulled her dress over her shoulders, and he helped as much as he could to lift it the rest of the way off. She gave it a gentle toss to the floor and straddled him, bare but for her panties, and looking into eyes that seemed distant for a moment. "Are you sure about this?" he rasped, his brows gathering.

He was giving her a way out, but she was in too deep now. Her body hummed from his touch and the promise of the pulsing manhood beneath her. She wanted more…she wanted it all.

She was the *new* Jess.

"I'm sure, Zane."

He nodded and blew out a breath in apparent relief, but there was something else. A part of him seemed undecided. It was only a feeling she had, a vibe that worried her in some small part of her consciousness. Don't think. Don't think. Don't think.

The new Jess wasn't a thinker. She was a doer.

She bent to his mouth, her sensitized nipples reaching his chest first. He bucked under her. "Oh, man, babe." She smiled at him and opened her mouth, coaxing his tongue to play with hers. His strokes made her dizzy, and her desire for him soared. She was almost ready. She reached for his zipper.

"No," he said. He gently rolled her to her side and leaned over her. "There might be something I'm good at with my left hand."

A smile broke out on her face, but Zane wiped the smile away the second his fingers probed inside her panties. He cupped her there, and a melodic sigh escaped her throat. He kissed her, swallowing the rest of her sounds as he stroked her with deft fingers. Her body moved, arched, reached as he became more and more merciless. "Zane," she cried.

She climbed over the top immediately, her limbs shaking, her breathing quickened and labored. A drawn-out, piercing scream rang from her throat. She was cocooned in heat. Zane held her patiently while her tingles ebbed and she came down to earth.

"Reach over to the bed stand, sweetheart," he said as she caught her breath. "Dig deep in the drawer." He nuzzled her ear and said softly, "It's been a while."

Seconds later, with a little of her help, he was sheathed. She reeled from the passion she witnessed in his eyes. It wasn't lust, but something more. Something she could feel good about when she remembered this night. They were connected, always had been, and right now all things powerful in the universe were pulling her toward this man.

"Ready?" he asked.

As she nodded, boldly she lifted her leg over his waist to straddle him. Both of his hands came around her back, encouraging her to lean down. She did, and he pressed a dozen molten kisses to her mouth before he set her onto him.

Instinctively she rose up, and he helped guide her down. The tip of his shaft teased her entrance, and she closed her eyes.

"So beautiful," she heard him say softly as he filled her body.

They moved together as one, his thrusts setting the pace. Her heart beat rapid-fire; she was in the Zane zone now and offered to him everything he wanted to take.

He was all she could ever hope for in a lover. His kiss drove her crazy, and he was more adept with one good hand than the men she'd known in the past who'd had the use of both. He explored her body with tender kisses and bold touches, with harmonious rhythm and unexpected caresses. He was wild and tender, sweet and wicked. And when he pressed her for finality that he seemingly couldn't hold back another second, her release astonished and satisfied her. "Wow," she whimpered, her body still buzzing. She lay sated and spent on the bed.

"Yeah, babe. Wow." Zane sighed heavily, an uncomplicated sound telling her how much pleasure she'd brought him. She wasn't sorry. She had no regrets. But then, she hadn't let her mind wander since she'd entered Zane's bedroom. She didn't want to think. Not now.

Zane wrapped his arm around her, tucking her into him, and soon the sound of his quiet breaths steadied. With all that he'd consumed tonight, there was no reason to hope that he would wake soon.

She closed her eyes, savoring the safety and serenity the night brought to her.

Zane's eyes snapped open to the ceiling above. It was funny how the crater-like texture seemed odd to him this morning. He'd never noticed it before. Back home, solid wood beams supported the house. The rich smell of pines and oaks and cedar lent warmth and gave him a true sense of belonging. He missed home, longed for it actually, but how in hell could he complain? He lived in a rich man's paradise, on a sandy windswept beach with dazzling pastel sunsets and beautiful people surrounding him.

He didn't have to look over to know Jess wasn't beside him on the bed. He'd heard her exit the room in the wee hours of the morning. He should've stopped her. He should've reached out and tugged her back to bed. If he had, she'd be here with him now, and he would nestle into her warmth again.

Sweet Jess. *Sexy Jess.*

Oxygen pushed out of his lungs. He was still feeling the effects of last night. The alcohol, the soft woman—the entire night played back in his mind. He was in deep now.

He hinged his body up and swiveled his feet over the bed to meet with the floor. He made a grab for his crutches that lay against the wall and luckily hung on to them. Rising, still wearing the pants he'd worn last night, he ambled from the bedroom to the living room. From there, he spotted Jess pressed against the deck railing in a pair of sexy shorts and a ruffled blouse, gazing out to sea. It was just after dawn, and the beach was empty but for a few seagulls milling about. Low curling waves splashed against the shore almost silently. It was a beautiful time of day.

Made even more beautiful by his golden-haired houseguest.

As quietly as a man on crutches could, he made his way out the double French doors and headed toward her. Her concentration was intense, and she didn't hear him approach until he was behind her. He put his crutches near the wall and braced his arms on the railing, trapping her in his embrace.

She stood with her back to his chest. Her hair whipped in the breeze and tickled his cheeks as he nibbled on her nape. She tasted like a woman who'd had a delicious night of sex. She smelled like a woman who'd been sated and well loved. He breathed her in. "Mornin', Jess."

"Hmm."

"Wish you hadn't left my bed. Wish you were still in there with me."

As she nodded, she leaned her head against his shoulder. "I don't know what we're doing," she said softly.

"Helping each other heal, maybe." He nipped the soft skin under her ear. "All I know is, I haven't felt this alive in a long time. And that's because of you."

"It's only because I remind you of—"

"Home." He wouldn't allow her to think for a second she was a replacement for his dead wife. He wasn't certain in his own mind that wasn't the case—her transformation last night had knocked the vinegar out of him, she'd looked so much like Janie—but he didn't want Jess believing it. What kind of a scoundrel would that make him? "But it's more than that. You remind me of the good things in my life."

"You're romanticizing about Beckon. It's really not all that."

In a way, they were both in the same situation. She'd had her heart broken. Of course she wouldn't look upon home with fond memories now. He couldn't go home because it wouldn't be the same. He blamed himself for Janie's death, and the guilt wracked him ten ways to Sunday, each and every day. "Maybe you're right, sweetheart."

Memories being what they were, he couldn't deny he held Beckon close to his heart. But he didn't need to win this round with Jessica today.

"I don't have a single regret about last night. Well, except that I had the damn boot and cast still on."

She turned away from the ocean and captured his attention with her pretty fresh-meadow eyes. "Not one, Zane? Not one regret?"

He blinked at the intensity of her question. This was important to her. "No."

What he had were doubts. He wasn't ready for anything heavy, with her or anyone else. The thought of entering into a relationship gave him hives. He might never be ready. He'd removed himself from any thoughts of the future and lived in the present. He'd shut himself off for two years. It was safe. His haven of sanity.

"Are you regretting what happened last night?" He wasn't sure he wanted to hear her answer.

Her chin lifted as she thought about it for an eternity of seconds. "*Regret* isn't the right word. I think you're right. We both needed each other."

"We don't have to attach any labels to last night," Zane said. "It just happened." He wanted it to happen again. But it wasn't his decision. He was smart enough to know that.

"But where do we go from here?"

Breezes blew her hair off her shoulders, the golden strands dancing in the morning light. Her face was clean of makeup, glowing with a fresh-washed look. All of Zane's impulses heightened.

"First," he said, dipping his head to her mouth, "I give you a good morning kiss." He pressed his lips to hers and kissed her soundly. She made a tiny noise in the back of her throat that made him smile inside. He could kiss her until the sun set and wouldn't tire of it. He inched away from her face as her eyes opened, glowing with warmth. God, she was sweet. "If you're inclined to do some cooking this morning, we have breakfast. Mrs. Lopez doesn't work on Sunday. And then we do whatever comes natural. No pressure, Jess."

He'd had sex with Janie's younger sister. He should be beating himself up about that now, but oddly he wasn't. He couldn't figure the why of it. Why was being with Jess making him feel better about himself instead of worse? He had nothing to offer her but strong arms to hold her and a warm body to comfort her, if she needed them. He couldn't pursue her. It wouldn't be fair to her, but that didn't stop him from wanting her.

A soft, relieved breath blew from her lips. "That sounds good to me, Zane." She gave him a sweet smile and handed him his crutches. "Meet me in the kitchen in half an hour."

His gaze landed on the curvy form of her backside as she strode inside the house. He hung his head. Oh, man. He was in deep.

Life at 211 Moonlight Drive wasn't going to get any easier.

Seven

Two and a half months after his accidental fall off a Los Angeles stage, Zane had gotten a good report from his doctor. His foot had healed nicely and was now out of the cast. His wrist had taken longer than expected to heal, but that, too, was in great shape and cast-free. Jessica was almost as relieved as he was, hearing the news today after driving him to his appointment. Zane had never gotten used to the crutches and now, with a little physical therapy, he'd be back to normal, good as new. And her duties wouldn't be so up close and personal with him any longer. She could concentrate on work and try to forget about making love with him two nights ago.

The new Jess would've let it go by now.

But traces of the old Jess were resurfacing, and she wanted to kick her to the curb. Falling in love with Zane would be a bonehead stupid move. He was still in love with Janie, and nothing much could persuade her otherwise. How could she be sure that the night they'd had sex wasn't more about her resemblance to her sister than any intense affection Zane had for her?

"I feel like celebrating," Zane said as she drove toward the gates of his home.

"I bet you do. But you can't go dancing just yet. You have to get through physical therapy."

From out of the corner of her eye, she spied Zane flexing his hand. "I'm fine. Just dandy. Even wearing my own boots for a change."

She took her eyes off the road for a split second to gaze at his expensive boots. Snakeskin. Gorgeous. Studded black leather. They made her mouth water. "You do know you live on the beach. Sandals are expected. Even admired."

A belly laugh rolled out of his mouth. "I could say the same about you. Lately, you've been wearing those high-falutin heels."

"Me?" Yes, it was true. The new Jess wore pricey heels when she wasn't in her morning walk tennis shoes.

"Yeah, you. Admit it. You're happier in a pair of soft leather boots with flat heels than those skyscrapers you've taken to wearing. Not that I mind. You look hot in those heels."

The compliment lit her up inside, but she couldn't let him see how it affected her. She lowered her sunglasses and gave him a deadpan look.

He grinned.

The man was in a great mood today, happier than she'd seen him in days. It was certainly better than putting up with his sourpuss, like on Sunday afternoon when he'd balked at her going to Dylan's house for the screening of *Time of Her Life*. She'd thought he'd be okay with it. After all, he'd said to do what came natural, and she had promised Dylan she'd be there. When she'd walked in past nine, missing dinner with him, he'd been sullen and distant, none too pleased with her.

Yes, they'd had sex the night before, and it had been amazing. Surely Zane had to know that Dylan McKay, handsome as he was, didn't strike her fancy. She'd gone because she'd promised and because she needed time away from Zane to clear her head, yet that entire afternoon and evening, she'd wondered if she'd made a mistake by going to Dylan's.

"You know what I feel like doing?" Zane asked, breaking into her thoughts.

"I'm afraid to ask."

"I feel like taking a dip."

"In your Jacuzzi? That's a good idea. I bet the warm water—"

"In the ocean, Jess. Tonight, after dinner."

She pulled through the gates and drove along the winding road to his house. "I don't know if that's wise, Zane. You shouldn't push it. You only just—"

"I'm going, Jess." He set his face stubbornly, and she couldn't think of anything to say to change his mind. "I've been confined long enough."

Pulling into the garage, she cut the engine. "I get that, but I won't be—"

Oh, shoot. He wasn't going to like this.

"Won't be what?"

"Home after dinner."

"Another shopping trip?"

A lie could fall from her lips very easily. But she wasn't going to lie to Zane. "No. I'm invited over to your neighbor's house."

Zane's lips thinned. "Dylan again?"

"Adam Chase."

Zane's eyes sharpened on her. "You're going over to Adam's tonight?"

"I kind of didn't give him a choice the other night. He was telling me about his new artwork, and I hinted at wanting to see it. I guess he was just being nice by inviting me over." She'd been a little stunned and humbled when he'd asked her since, according to Zane, invitations from Adam were rare.

Zane closed his eyes briefly. "That's Adam. Mr. Nice Guy."

"You don't think he is?"

Zane snorted. "I think he's a genius. But I don't know much about his personal life."

"I don't want to know about his personal life, either. This isn't anything, Zane." If only she could melt the disapproval off his face with an explanation. "It's just me, being curious. The teacher in me loves learning."

They'd been carefully dancing around what had happened between them. It seemed neither wanted to bring the subject up. So how could she admit that she'd rather be home with him? That after making love with him, it was better that they spend time apart. Too much alone time with him could prove disastrous. One disaster per decade was her limit. One disaster in her entire life would be preferable.

She cared deeply for Zane, thought he was gorgeous and more appealing than any man she'd ever met, but she couldn't be dumb again. And that meant not reading too much into having sex with him, wonderful as it was. She rationalized it was all about healing. Isn't that how Zane passed it off?

"I'm sure Adam wouldn't mind if you joined me."

He reached for the door handle. "I've seen his house, Jess. You go on. Have a nice time," he said through tight lips.

She didn't buy his comment for a second, but she clamped her mouth shut, and as he opened the car door, she rushed around the front end to meet him. Putting his good foot down, he braced his hands on the sides of the car and brought himself up and out.

"Lean on me," she said. "I'm here if you need me."

"I'll make it just fine."

She moved out of his way, and he walked slowly but on his own power, his boots scraping the garage floor as he made his way into the house.

Her shoulders fell, and black emptiness seemed to swallow her up. She wanted Zane to need her.

Or maybe, she just plain wanted Zane. Either way

wasn't an option. She couldn't very well count the days until Mariah returned. Nobody knew when that would be.

But for the first time, she hoped it would be soon.

Zane leaned his elbows over his deck banister, grateful to be on his own two feet now. His gaze focused on Jess as she made her way down the deck steps to the beach. "Bye, Zane. I won't be long."

Her sultry voice hammered inside his brain. It was unique, and he was beginning to hear the slight nuances that differed from her sister's. There was more sugary rasp and a lightness in her tone that made him think of only good things.

She held the straps of her heeled sandals up by two fingers and waved at him once her bare feet hit the sand. In her other hand, she held a flashlight to guide her way over to Adam's house. It wasn't too far, just about one hundred yards from back door to back door, but the half moon's light wasn't enough illumination on the darkened beach, so the flashlight was a good idea.

Her blond hair touched the top of a nipped-at-the-waist snowy white dress that flared out to just above her knees. She looked ethereal in a delicate way that would turn any man's head.

"Bye" he heard himself growl, and lifted his hand up, a semiwave back, watching her trudge through the sand and out of his line of vision.

She was determined to go, yet he'd noted a flicker in her eyes earlier, a moment of doubt as if she waited for him to tell her to stay. He wanted her, and his newly healed body was in a state of arousal around her most of the time now, but he held back. He let her go off to another man's house tonight instead of giving in to his lust.

Was he an idiot or being smart, for her sake?

His cell phone rang, and he plucked it from his pocket. It was probably Mariah. She'd been a saint, checking in and worrying about him when she was the one who needed the support. He'd had Jess send her flowers this morning to cheer her up.

He answered the ring. "Hello?"

"Hello, Zane. This is Mae."

His brows rose. It wasn't Mariah after all, but Jessica's mother. "Hi, Mae. This is a nice surprise."

"I hope so. Zane, how are you feeling these days?"

"Better. I'm out of my cast and healing up real good. And how are you, Mae?"

"I could be better. You know I'm an eternal worrier. And I'm worried about my Jess. I haven't heard from her in three days."

"Is that unusual?"

"Yes, very. She usually checks in with me every day or every other day. We've been playing phone tag over the weekend, and I can't seem to reach her. She didn't answer my call today. I wondered if something was wrong with her phone. Thought it'd be best to check in with you."

"Well…I can assure you, she's doing fine."

"Really?"

"Yes, ma'am."

"That's a relief. I thought after I gave her the news, she'd be crushed. My dear girl has been through a lot this past month. She can't be happy about Steven."

Steven? Just hearing the guy's name made his hand ball into a fist. "What news is that, Mae?"

"I couldn't hide it from my sweet girl. She didn't need to hear it from anyone else but her mama."

"Yes, I think you were right." Zane hadn't a clue what she was getting at, but he knew Mae. She'd eventually get around to telling him what was going on.

"Can you imagine her bridesmaid, Judy, running off with Steven to get married? Why, she'd been like a member of our family when the girls were younger. And Steven? I thought I knew that boy. I'd like to wallop both of them for the hurt they put my daughter through."

His face tightened and he squeezed his eyes shut, wishing like hell he could give that jerk a piece of his mind. And to add to the insult, he'd run away with one of Jess's good friends. A woman who'd vowed to stand up for her at her wedding.

Something clicked in his head. "Wait a minute, Mae. When did you tell Jess about this?"

"Oh, let me see. It must have been on Thursday. Yes, that's right. I remember, because I was getting my hair done at the salon and, well, it was the talk of the entire beauty shop. I felt so bad when I heard, I walked out after my cut with a wet head, didn't bother having my hair styled. All I kept thinking about was my Jess and how she would take the news. But you know, when I told her, I was surprised at her reaction. She seemed calm. I think she was in shock. Have you noticed anything different about her, lately?"

Had he? Hell, yeah. Now he understood her transformation. She'd dyed her hair blond, gotten rid of her eyeglasses, starting wearing provocative clothes. Was it rebellion? Or worse yet, had Jess decided to throw caution to the wind and… No, he wouldn't let his mind go there. She wasn't promiscuous. She was a woman who'd been betrayed by people she trusted. He could only imagine what hearing that news did to her.

And what had he done? She'd come into the room the night of party and he'd shot her down, doing the unthinkable by telling her she looked like Janie in a voice that held nothing but disapproval. He'd been selfish, thinking only about how much it hurt to look at her that way. If he was damn honest with himself, seeing that daring side of Jess had excited him. He hadn't known how to handle his initial reaction to her. She almost didn't go to the party because he'd given her a hard time about the way she looked, gorgeous as she was.

And he'd been jealous because he couldn't have her, and yet he didn't want any other man going after her, either. Wow. What a revelation.

"Zane, I asked if Jessica has been acting differently lately?"

Uh, yeah. But in this case, he saw no reason not to bend the truth a little. "She's been keeping busy, Mae. She tells me she likes the work. And she's made a few friends here, too. She seems to fit in real nice. In fact, she's visiting my neighbor now. When she comes in, I'll be sure to tell her you called."

"I'm happy about that, Zane. I knew coming to stay with you would be good for her."

Zane scrunched his face up. He'd taken Mae's daughter to bed, and if he had his way, he would do so again. His mind muddied up, and he didn't understand any of it other than that Jess was under his roof and getting under his skin. He felt for her and the hurt she'd gone through. Nothing about liking her seemed wrong, even though he could count the bullet points in his mind why he shouldn't.

"I can't thank you enough. You know how much I love my girls."

Her comment dug deep into his heart. Mae would never stop loving Janie. She always spoke of her as if she were still with them. Zane loved that about her. "Yep, I know, Mae."

"So tell me what you've been doing. That's if you have the time."

"I have the time. Let's see, the restaurant is coming along as scheduled and…"

Thirty minutes later, after he'd hung up with Mae, he sat down with his guitar and strummed lightly to reacquaint himself to the feel of the instrument in his hands and the resiliency of the strings. He had words in his head struggling to get out, lyrics that were just beginning to flow, and he jotted them down as he struck chord after chord. The pick in his hand felt awkward at first, but he pressed on.

Thoughts of Jess distracted him. He couldn't stop thinking about her and what Mae had revealed. He wanted to protect her. Yet he desired her. Her heartache scored his heart. He felt sorry for her, but not enough to keep his distance. He was *conflicted*, as Dylan would say. He needed some release.

Only a dunk in the ocean would help clear his mind and cool his body.

And minutes later, dressed in his swim trunks, he made his way to the shoreline and dived straight in, propelling his arms and legs past the shallow waters, pushing his body to the limit.

After enjoying a pleasant visit with Adam and declining his offer to walk her home, she trudged across the beach alone. Cool sand squished between her toes as she made her way to the shoreline, where the moist grains under her feet became smoother, making it much easier to move. She knew this beach; she'd walked it in the mornings many times.

As she entered Zane's home, silence surrounded her. It was too quiet for this time of the evening. Zane never turned in before ten. "Zane? Are you here?"

Nothing.

"Zane?" She stepped into the office, then the kitchen, and peeked into his bedroom.

There was no sign of him.

She sighed wearily and shook her head. He must have gone for a swim in the ocean. Half a dozen worries entered her head about his night swim. Geesh, he'd just gotten his cast off. What was the doggone rush?

Hurrying to her room, she flung off her clothes and put on her bathing suit. In her haste to rid herself of the old Jess, she'd tossed out her one-piece swimsuits she'd brought from Texas, which left her with the daring bikini she'd bought the other day. She slipped into it and then wiggled a T-shirt over her head. Without wasting a second, she strode down the stairs, grabbed her flashlight and ventured out the sliding door.

If she were lucky, she'd find Zane walking toward the house, whistling a happy tune.

Who was she kidding? Luck wasn't with her lately. Zane's towel was on the beach, which meant he was out there somewhere. The crashing waves that usually lulled her to sleep made her wary now. Her flashlight pointed out to sea illuminated only a narrow strip of water at a time. She squinted, trying to make out shapes, searching corridors of ocean, back and forth. "Zane! Zane!"

She couldn't find him. Nibbling her lip, she paced the beach, aiming her flashlight onto the water over and over. She'd never swum in the ocean before coming to California, but she'd quickly learned how the currents could take you away, making you drift in one direction or another. She'd start out in front of Zane's house and wind up hundreds of feet away when it was time to come in. Those currents had to be stronger at night, more powerful and…

She spotted something. A head bobbing in the water? She pointed the flashlight and struggled to focus. Yep, someone was out there. But then the form dropped down as if being swallowed up by the sea. She ran into the surf, targeting that bit of water with the flashlight. "Zane!" she shouted, but her voice was muted by the crash of the waves.

He couldn't hear her. He was out past the shallows. She waited several long seconds for him to reappear. She prayed that he would. She couldn't see much, only what the moonlight and stars and her flashlight allowed, but she'd always had a good sense of direction. She knew the exact spot where she'd seen him go down.

"Oh, God. Zane!"

With no time to waste, she dived in, her arms pumping, her feet kicking, fighting against the tide. She swam as fast as she ever had in her life, her eyes trying to focus on the spot she'd seen him. She was almost there, a little farther, just another few strokes.

A thunderous sound boomed in her ears. She looked up. Oh, no. A monstrous wave was coming toward her like a coiling snake. It was too late to get out of its path. The pounding surf reached her in midstroke. The force slammed her back. She flew in the air and belly-flopped facedown against a sheet of ocean as hard as a slab of granite.

Waves buried her, and she sputtered for breath.

Seconds later, she felt herself being lifted, her head popping above the water. She gasped.

"Jess."

Zane. He'd come for her. How did he get here? As she struggled to catch her breath, he half dragged, half swam her to the shallows by floating on his back and keeping her head above water. Once he got his footing, he stopped and stood upright in the water, then scooped her into his arms, carrying her to the beach.

He laid her down carefully away from high tide. The sand granules scratched at her back, but she was never happier to be on dry land. And Zane was safe. That mattered just as much.

He fell to his knees beside her. Huffing breaths, he shook his head. "You gave me a scare."

He bent to her, pushing aside the locks of hair hiding her face, and his magnificent eyes were soft and concerned. "Are you okay?"

She nodded. "I'm okay. Got the wind knocked out of me."

"You almost drowned, sweetheart. What on earth were you doing?"

She filled her lungs with oxygen, this time without gulping water along with it. "Saving you," she said quietly. "I thought I saw you out there, going under."

Zane's eyes were warm on her face, the heat enough to keep the cool drops on her body from freezing. His hands were working wonders, too, caressing her cheeks and stroking her chin, heating her up in ways no other man ever had. He rasped softly, "You mean you thought I was drowning, and you risked your life to save me?"

She nodded.

"That wasn't me, sweetheart."

"It wasn't? I saw someone go under. I thought for sure you were out there."

"I was. I lasted only ten minutes before I came in. What you saw was probably a school of sea lions. They frequent the shallower waters here at night. I've seen one of them pop a head up and then go under and, yeah…I guess in the dark, it might look like a swimmer out there."

"Then how…how did you find me?"

"After my swim, I took a long walk. Thankfully, I returned just in time to hear you calling my name. Took me only a second to figure out where you were."

He began to rub her arms and legs. She was cold, but that didn't stop her from reacting to his touch. As warmth spread through her body, her gentle cooing seemed to draw Zane's attention to her lips. "That feels good," she said.

"Tell me about it." The corner of his mouth crooked up.

His palms heated her through and through, her skin highly sensitized to his touch. She was overwhelmed with relief that he hadn't drowned and grateful that he'd saved her, but there was more…so much more that she was feeling right now. "Thank you, Zane."

She touched his shoulder and felt his cool skin under her fingertips. His eyes gleamed with a fiery invitation to do more. Bravely, she wound her arms around his neck. It didn't take an ounce of effort to pull him close. His mouth hovered near hers.

It was crazy. They were on the beach under the moonlight and dripping wet after the rescue, and nothing seemed amiss in her world. She wouldn't trade places with another living soul right now.

"I'd give you what-for," he said, "but that will have to wait."

"It will?"

"Yep. Cause I think you're about to kiss me."

"Smart man."

She ran her fingers through his thick wet hair and lowered his head down to her lips. Oh…he tasted warm and inviting and salty. His kiss made her tremble in a good way, and she opened her mouth for him.

He plunged inside and swept her up in one burning kiss after another. What was left of her body when he finished kissing her was a pulsing bundle of need. "Zane," she whispered over his lips.

"I need to get you inside the house…"

He didn't have to finish. She knew. They'd get arrested if they acted on their impulses right here on the beach.

"Can you walk?" he asked.

"Yes, with your help."

"Okay, sweetheart. Seems one of us is always leaning on the other."

She smiled. How true.

He bounded up and then entwined their hands. Gently he helped her to her feet. The world didn't go dizzy on her—well, except for the hot looks Zane was giving her. "I actually feel pretty good."

"Glad to hear it." He kissed her earlobe. "Ready?"

"Ready."

Side by side, bracing each other, they walked through the sand and up the steps that led into the house.

As soon as they entered the house, Zane did an about-face and walked her backward until she was pressed against the living room wall. He trapped her there, his body pulsing near hers, his gaze generating enough heat to burn the building down.

"Are you about to give me what-for?"

A low rumble of laughter rose from his throat. Her senses heightened. He was one sexy man. "You know it, Jess." He glanced down at her dripping wet T-shirt plastered to her body and sighed as if he was in pain. "Do you know how incredibly perfect you are?"

His hands wrapped around her waist, and thrilling warmth penetrated through her shirt to heat her skin. "I'm not."

His mouth grazed her throat. "You are. You can't let what those two did to you change who you are. That guy was about the stupidest man on earth."

She stilled. "What do you mean, 'those two'?"

Zane's lips were doing amazing things to her throat. And his body pressing against hers made it hard to think. Her breasts were ready for his touch. Her nipples pebbled hard and beckoned him through the flimsy T-shirt and bikini.

She had to ignore her body. She needed to know what he meant. "Zane?"

He stopped kissing her and inched away enough to gaze into her eyes. "Oh, uh. Your mama called while you were out. She was worried about you, and well…she told me about Steven running off with a friend of yours."

She'd told him about Judy?

All the wind left her lungs, and a different kind of burn seared through her stomach. She wished Mama hadn't revealed to Zane her latest humiliation. She felt so exposed, so vulnerable. Did she have an ounce of pride left?

"You have every right to feel hurt, Jess. But don't let what he did change the person that you are."

"You think that's what I'm doing?"

"Isn't it? You changed your hair, wear your contacts all the time. You dress differently now. Don't get me wrong. You look beautiful, sweetheart. But you were beautiful before."

She shrugged. She found it hard to believe. It was a platitude, a cliché, a way to make her feel better about herself.

"I need the change." Tears misted in her eyes. She really did. She needed to look at herself in the mirror and see a strong, independent woman who had style and confidence. She needed to see that transformation, more than anything else.

"I get that." Zane took her into his arms and hugged her, as a friend now. She felt safe again, protected. And just being with him made her problems seem trivial. "But promise me one thing?"

"What?"

"Don't try to find what you need with another man. Makes me crazy."

Makes me crazy. Oh, wow. There was no mistaking what he meant. Not from the genuine pain she found in his eyes, or the intensity in his voice. "You mean like Dylan or Adam? I told you, they're not—"

He shushed her with a kiss, right smack on the lips. Her body instantly reacted, and goose bumps rose on her arms.

"*You* make me crazy, too," he rasped and began rolling the hem of her T-shirt up. With his coaxing, she raised her arms as he brought the wet garment over her head and her breasts jiggled back into place. Zane's hot gaze touched her there and lingered, then traveled over the rest her body clad in a skimpy New Jess bikini. He made a loud noise from sucking oxygen into his lungs. "From now on, sweet Jess, I want to be the man you go to when you need something."

"You mean, like my rebound guy?"

"Call it whatever you want, honey."

Jess didn't have to think twice. Zane just abolished all deprecating thoughts she'd had about herself and totally wiped out any pain she'd felt about Steven. Even her pride was restored somewhat. The Steven ship had sailed, and she wasn't going to waste another second thinking of him. Not when she had Zane offering her the moon.

He was a real man.

If she had any doubts before about her feelings for him,

they were banished the second she'd thought he was drowning. She'd rushed in to save him, praying that God wouldn't take him from her. And she wasn't going to feel bad about it or apologize to anyone. Forbidden or not, she wanted him.

"I promise."

He hooked his fingers with hers. "Your room or mine?"

"Neither," she said. Her confidence soaring and her heart melting, she let go of every inhibition she'd ever had. "I think we need a hot, steamy shower to warm up, don't you?"

"As long as I get to peel this bikini off you, you've got yourself a deal."

Eight

The peeling was blissful torture. Jessica lay her head against cool slate, her arms behind her. Steam rose up as the customized shower streams poured down, warming her bones. It was like being tucked inside a large waterfall, cascading water all around her. Zane came to her naked, his sculpted, bronzed beach body equal to that of an ancient god. There was enough room for twelve people in the master shower, but she knew Zane would make good use of the space for the two of them.

"You're beautiful, Jess."

His mouth covered hers as both of his hands came under her bikini top. Weighing her full breasts, he groaned deep in his throat, and his appreciation of her body flowed to her ears. She roped her arms around his neck and continued to kiss him even as he unhooked the back of the bathing suit, releasing her breasts. Warm spray moistened them and he worked magic on her, gliding his hands over her bare, wet skin and arousing her in tortuous increments. His thumb caressed her already pebbled nipples until she muted a cry.

He was amazingly gentle, but brutal in his determination to make it good for her. As he removed the bottom half of her bikini, his hands shaking with need, she'd never felt more desirable and powerful.

Drizzling kisses along her throat, his hands came to the small of her back, and she bowed her body for him. He took one jutted breast in his mouth and suckled her, his tongue swirling and flicking. She screamed then, but the pleasured sounds were drowned out by the thunderous showerheads. He gave the other breast equal treatment, and it was almost too much.

"Are you warm yet?" he asked, nuzzling her throat.

"Just getting there."

"Let me help you with that."

He picked up a bar of soap and lathered her from head to toe, bathing her in a soft and subtle flowery scent that reminded her of a spring afternoon. He didn't miss one inch of her, paying special attention to the crux of her womanhood, stroking, washing, cupping her, making her moan. "Oh, oh, oh."

Jess thought every woman should experience a shower this way, just once.

She smiled, gritted her teeth and savored the pleasure he brought her.

His hands moved to her backside and slid over the rounded halves of her derriere, molding her form, spreading his fingers wide as if savoring the feel of her. His manhood pressed her belly, rock-hard and pulsing. She shuddered, unable to hold back another second. Her body released gently, in beautifully timid waves that nudged her forever toward him. His mouth covered hers, and she enjoyed the sweetly erotic taste of his passion.

Wow.

She'd never had an orgasm like that before.

She clung to him and let the full force of her feelings consume her.

"Did you like that, sweetheart?"

"So much."

She sensed his smile, and it made her heart nearly burst.

She moved down on him, letting her mouth and breasts caress the middle of his chest, his belly, and then she touched his full-fledged erection.

"Oh, man," he uttered. "Jess."

He fisted a handful of her hair and helped move her along the length of him. Water pounded her back, the showerhead pulsing now. It was deliciously sexy, and when she was through, she rose to meet him. The hungry look on his face, teeth gritted, eyes gleaming like a wolf about to devour his prey, would have been almost frightening if it wasn't Zane.

He lifted her, and on instinct she wrapped her legs around his waist. He held her tight and murmured, "Hang on."

She clung to him, and his manhood nudged into her, filling her with gentle force. He was patient and oh, so ready. She moved on him, letting him know she was okay with whatever he wanted to do. The beat, beat, beat of the raining drops set the pace of his thrusts. He arched and drove deeper.

"Oh." She sighed. "So good."

He kissed her throat, her breasts, and continued to thrust into her, hard, harder.

It was pure heaven. She'd never made love like this before. Her heart pounded in her chest, and her body soared. Spasms of tight, sweet pain released, and she cried out softly "Oh, Zane."

His eyes were on her, burning hot. He waited for her to come down off the clouds, and then he began to thrust into her again. He set a fast rhythm, and she gave back equally. She wanted to make it good for him, too.

Guttural groans rose up his throat, and she knew he was close. He impaled her one last, amazing time, his reach touching the very core of her womanhood. And waves of his orgasm struck her, one after the other, until he was spent, sated.

He took her with him as he sat down on the stone shower bench, raining kisses all over her face, cheeks, chin, throat. He pushed her hair away from her face. "Are you okay, sweetheart?"

How could she not be? She was overjoyed. "It was beautiful, Zane."

"It was," he said, leaning way back.

She stroked his face, running her hand over his stubbly cheek. He grabbed her wrist and planted a kiss on her palm.

The shower turned off. Perfect timing. It was a perfect night. Well, except for those few minutes she thought Zane was drowning. He'd taxed his body tonight. "You must be tired," she said.

His eyes darkened, and he hiked a brow. "I'm ready to be in bed with you."

"Sounds good."

She didn't want the night to end. She no longer worried about what tomorrow would bring. She was living in the moment, and these moments had been pretty darn spectacular.

Zane lifted her off him and grabbed two giant towels. He took his time drying her off, sneaking kisses on parts of her body, arousing her. She did the same to him, teasing him with her mouth.

They entered his bedroom clean, dry and exhausted.

She took a few steps toward his door, and his arm snaked around her. "Where do you think you're going?"

"To my room. I need to get my nightie."

"No, you don't. Come to bed. I promise to keep you warm."

"Part of your duties as my rebound guy?"

"You know it, honey. Now get in."

Spooning with Zane in his big, comfortable bed, Jessica's eyes eased open. It was slightly after dawn, and the usual early morning cloud cover allowed a smidgen of struggling sunshine into the room. Zane stroked her hip, lightly, possessively, his touch becoming familiar to her, and she purred like a kitten given a big bowl of cream.

"I'm giving you the day off," he murmured, his breath whispering over her hair.

"Mmm." A lovely thought. "I have work to do today."

"It'll keep, Jess. I want to spend the day with you."

"You already do."

He nipped her earlobe, then planted tiny kisses along her nape. His hand traveled deliciously to her waist, just under her belly. "Not the way I want to."

They'd made love twice last night. It was incredible and frightening at the same time. Every so often, thoughts of her future would break through her steely resolve to live in the moment. She'd shudder, and sudden panic would set in. What was she doing? Where was all this leading? They hadn't used protection in the shower last night, but Jess was on birth control, sort of. She'd skipped a few days during the height of her wedding fiasco, but she'd resumed when she'd arrived here to keep her hormones from getting out of whack.

She turned to Zane, roping her arms around his neck. "What did you have in mind?"

He kissed her quickly and then tugged her closer. "A day of play. We can get out of here. Have fun."

A lock of his thick hair fell to his forehead. In many ways, he looked like a little boy, eager to play hooky. He lived in this dream house on the beach and spoke of getting away, as if he'd been in living in the slums all this time. The irony made her smile, and she toyed with that wayward lock of hair, curling it around her finger, mesmerized by the man she shared a bed with.

"You're the boss," she whispered.

"I'm not your boss," he said softly. "Not when it comes to this."

He began kissing her shoulder, her throat, her chin. And then he stopped suddenly and inched away. He shot her a solid, earnest look. "Would you like to spend the day with me?"

Oh, wow. Like a date? "Yes." She yanked the lock of hair. "Of course, silly."

He gave her backside a gentle squeeze. "Then we'd better get up and get showered. You first. If we share another shower, we'll never make it out of here this morning." He waggled his brows. "On second thought, maybe…"

She laughed and jumped out of bed. "I'm going in first."

Less than an hour later, Zane was sitting behind the wheel of his SUV and pulling out of the gates of his home. "Feels good to be driving again. I hated feeling helpless, having to rely on someone to take me places."

A few days of stubble on his face had led to a short, sexy beard. The new look turned her on. Everything about him seemed to do that. All she had to do was think about making love with him last night and tingles fluttered inside her belly.

He wore a baseball cap instead of his Stetson. The beard and sunglasses also helped disguise him. He'd healed so well, she would've never guessed he'd broken his foot, except for his slight limp as he tried not to put too much pressure on it. She already knew she'd be arguing with him about going to his rehab appointments.

He'd told her to wear her boots, dress in jeans and not question where they were going. He wanted to surprise her. She sat in her comfortable clothes, watching the stunning landscape go by as they left the blue waters behind and drove up a mountain road. The scenery lent itself to light conversation and soft music. Zane sang along with the tune on the radio, his voice deep and rich, her own personal concert. She couldn't help but grin.

Thirty minutes later, they were atop the mountain at a sprawling ranch-style home overlooking the city to the south and the valley to the north. The air was clean up here, the smog of the day blown away by ocean breezes. "Where are we?" she asked.

"My friend Chuck Bowen owns this place with his mother. It's called Ruby Ranch."

She glanced around and spotted white-fenced corrals, vineyards off in the distance and acres and acres of hilly, tree-dotted land. The sound of horses whinnying and snorting reached her ears.

"C'mon."

Zane exited the car and walked around to help her out. He took her hand. That little boy excitement once again lit his expression. "We're going riding."

"Riding?" She hadn't been on a horse since she was a teenager. She'd go riding every weekend with her good friend Jolie Burns when she wasn't working at Holcomb House. Jolie lived on a cattle ranch ten miles outside of Beckon. Jessica had the use of a pretty palomino named Sparkle, and she'd learned how to wash down and groom a horse back then, too. It was expected. If you exercised a horse, got him lathered up, then it was your responsibility to see to his needs after the ride. Jessica had fallen in love with Sparkle. She never minded the hard work that came with him.

She rubbed her hands together. This could be fun. "Oh, boy!"

Zane chuckled and kissed the tip of nose. "That's what I thought."

A fiftysomething woman with hair the color of deep, rich red wine walked out of the house. She was flawless in her appearance, neat and tidy, and her pretty face must have stopped men in their tracks when she was younger. Even now, she was stunning and dressed in Western clothes that looked as if they'd just come off a fashion runway.

"Hi, Ruby," Zane said.

"Zane. It's good to see you again."

Zane took Jessica's hand as he moved toward the house. Ruby tried not to react, but her eyes dipped to their interlocked hands for a second before she gave them both a smile. "Ruby, I'd like you to meet Jessica Holcomb. Jess, this is Ruby Bowen. She and Chuck own this amazing land."

They came to a stop on her veranda. "Hello," Jessica said. "The place is lovely. You have vineyards?"

"Thank you. Yes, we grow grapes and raise horses. It's a rare mix, but it works for Chuck and me. We don't bottle the wine here—we're too small for that—but we do have our own label. It's fun, hectic and keeps us plenty busy."

"I bet," Jessica said.

"I met Ruby and Chuck at a charity auction six months ago," Zane said. "Being original Texans, they've been gracious enough to offer their stables for whenever I wanted to ride."

"Absolutely. We've got over a thousand acres and plenty of horses that need exercising. We figured Zane was like a fish out of water, living at the beach these days. We're happy he took us up on the offer. Chuck's out of town and due back later. He'll be sorry he missed you. But please, make use of the grounds. The stables are just down the hill a ways. Our wrangler, Stewie, is waiting for you. He'll find a good fit for both of you."

"Thanks, Ruby. Would've been by sooner, but it's hard to ride with a broken foot and wrist. Just recently got the dang cast off."

"Well, you're here now, and that's all that matters. Have a good time. Be sure to stop by afterward. Chuck may be home by then."

"Will do, and thanks again," Zane said.

Just minutes later, Jessica rode atop a sweet bay mare named Adobe, and Zane sat a few hands taller on a black gelding named Triumph. In her hometown of Beckon, the terrain was flat as the tires in Jeb's Junkyard. But here at Ruby Ranch, set in the Santa Monica Mountains, the powder-blue sky seemed nearly touchable. They ambled along a path that led away from the house into land that rose high and dipped gently alongside a creek.

"No rain lately," Zane offered. "I bet this creek was a rushing stream at one time."

"It's still pretty awesome up here."

"It is. You miss riding?"

She nodded, holding on to the silver-gray felt hat Ruby's wrangler had offered her. Zane kept his ball cap on his head, but there was no doubt he was a cowboy, through and through. He may have great wealth and live in a contemporary beach house, but you couldn't take Texas out of a Texan. And that was fact. "I do. I love horses."

Zane gave a nod of agreement. "Yeah, me, too."

It was a sore subject and one Jess didn't want to press at the moment. Zane had abandoned his home after the fire that took Janie and their unborn baby's life. The place still stood as it was. Acres and acres of land gated off, going to waste. He hadn't had the heart to demolish what was left of his house or improve upon the land. He'd had an agent sell off the livestock, and that was that.

Heartbroken, Zane had picked up roots, leaving memories he couldn't deal with behind. Losing him had taken a big chunk out the hearts of the fine people of Beckon. Zane was their golden boy, a singer whose talent brought him great fame. The townsfolk were darn proud of their hometown hero. He'd had no more loyal fans in the world.

"I'm glad you brought me up here, Zane."

He eyed her, studying her face as if trying to puzzle something out. "I'd have never come without you. Fact is, Chuck's been after me to ride for months, and I never took him up on it." His voice seemed sort of strange, and then he took a giant swallow. "I didn't want to, until now."

She shouldn't read too much into it, but her heart jumped in her chest anyway. Hope could be just as drastic as despair to her right now. She shoved it away and took a different approach. "You were confined a long time. I bet getting up on a horse and riding is just what you needed. It's freeing."

"Maybe," he said. His index finger pushed at the corner of his mouth, contemplating. He gave his head a shake. "Maybe it's something else. Having to do with you."

Oh, God. Out in the open air, in these beautiful surroundings, anything seemed possible. *Don't hope. Don't hope.* "Me?"

He slowed his horse to a stop.

She did the same.

His dark eyes grazed her face. "Yeah, you," he said, his voice husky.

Her cheeks burned, and she hoped her new suntan along with the brim of her hat hid her emotions. Zane didn't need another groupie. They'd already established he was her rebound guy, whatever that really meant. She was his bed partner, for sure. But after that…she had no clue where she stood with him.

Maybe her crazy heart didn't want to know. Maybe she couldn't survive another disappointment. It was better not knowing, not thinking at all.

She clicked the heels of her boots and took off. "Race you to that plateau up ahead. First one to the oak tree wins!" She was already three lengths ahead of him when she heard his laughter.

"You're on!"

Westerly winds blew cool air at her face, her hair a riotous mess, as she leaned low on her mare and pressed the animal faster. The path was wide enough here for two horses, but branches hung low, and she expertly navigated through a thick patch of trees to reach the innermost edge of the clearing. Another fifty yards to go.

From behind, resounding hooves beat the ground, and she sensed Zane catching up.

"C'mon girl!" The mare was shorter, her legs not quite as long as Triumph's, and of course, Jessica was rusty as a rider.

It was a valiant effort, even if she'd cheated at the starting line, but Zane caught her. His gelding made the pass just five yards out, and yet Adobe wrestled to move faster. Her mare didn't like to lose, it seemed. They reached the oak tree, Triumph just nosing Adobe out.

Jess reined her mare in and circled around to the base of the oak tree. Zane sat atop his horse, grinning wide. His joy seared her heart. He was so dang happy. How could she not join in?

He dismounted and sauntered over to her, his confident strides stealing her breath. His recovery looked damn good on him, the smile on his face, the gleam in his eyes, the breadth of his shoulders...

"I win, Jess."

"Just barely." She gave a good fight.

"Still, a win is a win."

He reached up and helped her off, his large hands handling her with ease as she slid down the length of him. Tucked close, she didn't mind being in his trap. The exhilaration of the race and the handsomest darn face she'd ever seen brought on palpitations. Her heart pounded like crazy.

"So what do I win?" he asked.

"Is this a trick question?"

"Not even close."

"What do you want?"

A soap-opera villain couldn't have produced a more wicked grin. "A kiss, for starters."

"For starters?" Her gaze darted to his beautiful mouth, and a delicious craving began to develop. She didn't think she could play coy. She wanted him to kiss her, more than anything.

He nodded and bent his head. The second his yummy lips met hers, her mind rewound to last night and how his mouth had trailed pleasure all over her body. He'd tasted every inch of her. "Oh," she squeaked.

She sensed his smile from her noisy outburst as he continued to kiss her. Then he plucked the hat from her head and angled his mouth over hers again and again.

Backing up an inch, she gulped air to catch her breath and gazed into his mischievous eyes.

"You cheated in the race, sweetheart. You're gonna have to pay for that."

A dozen illicit notions popped into her head regarding how he'd make her pay, and a hot thrill spread like wildfire in her belly.

He tugged on her hand, and she followed as he led her behind the solid base of the sprawling oak tree. Hidden by drooping branches and fully shaded by overlapping leaves, he sat down, his back to the tree, and spread his legs. "Sit." He gestured to the place between his legs. "Relax."

Hardly a position that would have her relaxing, but she sat down, facing out, and rested her head on his chest. His arms wrapped around her, and he whispered in her ear, "Comfortable?"

She snuggled in deeper, her butt grazing his groin. A groan rose from his throat, and she chuckled. "Very."

His hands splayed across her ribcage. "Close your eyes."

She did.

"Now for your punishment."

He began to kiss the back of her neck, but it was what his hands were doing that made her dizzy. Deftly the tips of his fingers glided just under her breasts. Through the rough plaid material of her shirt, her nipples puckered in anticipation of his next move.

The snaps of her blouse popped open, his doing, and a startled gasp exploded from her lungs. "Zane!"

He brought his head around and kissed the corner of her mouth. "Shh. I'm pretty sure we're alone out here, but just in case, keep your shrieks to a minimum."

"You mean there's going to be more?"

He laughed quietly. Dipping into her bra, he flicked the pads of his thumbs over her responsive nipples. Her mouth opened, and he immediately stymied her next shriek with another kiss. "You are a loud one."

"You didn't mind last night," she breathed. He was doing amazing things to her with his hands.

"I don't mind now, but we're not on my turf anymore."

Damn it. She was his turf. It was becoming clearer and clearer to her. "So, maybe we should stop before someone sees us?"

"No one's out here, Jess. But I'll stop if you want me to. And that would be *my punishment*. I didn't think I could go all day without touching you again."

With a confession like that, how in the world could she tell him to stop? "You won, fair and square, Zane. I'm a big girl. I can take whatever you dish out."

Nine

"I like playing hooky with you," Zane said to Jessica over dinner at an exclusive, out-of-the-way nightspot overlooking the beach. He'd heard about this place from his neighbors, who commended the food, the privacy and the music. He sat beside her in a booth, listening to smooth jazz from a sax player with a powerful set of lungs.

Every time his gaze landed on Jessica tonight, he was reminded of the way she fell apart in his arms under that oak tree this morning. He hadn't planned on taking it as far as he did, but there was something about Jess that made him do wild things.

Maybe it was the sweet, squeaky sounds she sighed when he kissed her.

Or maybe it was the forbidden lust that came over him when she entered a room.

Or maybe it was her vulnerability and her honesty that drew him to her the most.

Those sexy shaves she'd given him didn't hurt, either.

"I like playing hooky with you, too." Her deep, sultry tone fit the atmosphere in the nightclub, reminding him every second he needed to finish what he'd started up on that plateau today.

She wore red tonight, a daring dress with a scoop neckline, the hem hiking up inches above her knees. The dress fit each sumptuous curve of her form to perfection. There were times when he forgot who she was, that he'd been married to Jessica's sister and that she wasn't ready for another relationship. He was her go-to guy, and he'd wanted it that way, but where it led from here, he didn't know. He didn't think past the present these days. He couldn't hope, didn't want to hope for more. He'd been sliced up pretty badly when Janie and his child died. The guilt ate at him every day.

He raised his wineglass and sipped, turning his gaze to the scant number of people dancing. He hadn't disguised himself tonight. He'd relied on the dimly lit surroundings and the back booth to keep his privacy. Sometimes his fame came at too high a price, and tonight he wanted to show Jess a good time. He wanted to hold her again. He roped his arm around her shoulder and spoke into her ear. "Dance with me?"

Her gaze moved to the dance floor and the amber hues focusing on couples sharing the spotlight. Yearning entered her eyes, and he'd be damned not to deliver her this little bit of pleasure.

"Are you sure?"

"Positive."

He rose and grabbed her hand, leading her to the center of the room. As soon as he stepped foot on the wood floor, he turned and tugged her to his chest. She fit him, her curves finding his angles, and they moved as if they were born to dance together.

"How's your foot?" she asked.

"It's floating on air right now. Fact is, both feet aren't touching the ground."

She chuckled. "Sweet, but I'm serious. You rode today, and now you're dancing."

"Thank you for your concern." He kissed her temple. "But I'm fine. Feels darn good doing some normal things again. And with the most beautiful woman in the room."

"How do you know? Have you checked all the other women out?"

"I, uh...not going to answer that one."

"Smart man."

He laughed, wrapping his arms tighter around her slim waist. Her breasts touched his chest, and he imagined her nipples pebbling for him, hardening through the delicate lace of her dress. Her hand wove through his hair, her fingertips playing with the strands as her arm lay on his shoulder, and it was the most intimate thing she'd done to him this entire day. His groin tightened instantly, and he backed away from her, fearing they'd get thrown out for an X-rated dance. Her gaze lifted, and pools of soft pasture green questioned him.

He shrugged, helpless.

She smiled then, and nodded.

He and Jess were on the same wavelength lately. They *got* each other, and everything felt right when he held her in his arms. He wasn't ready to let that feeling go. Luckily, he didn't have to think about that now.

Two dances later, they noticed their meals were being delivered to their table.

"Ready for dinner?"

Jessica nodded. "I think I've worked up an appetite."

"For food?"

"Among other things."

Jessica scooted into the booth, and he took his seat beside her as the waiter set down plates of pasta and petite loaves of garlic bread. Jess had chosen penne with sweet pesto sauce, and he'd ordered linguine with meat sauce. Steam rose up, the air around them flavored with spicy goodness.

"Looks heavenly," Jess said, picking up her fork.

"Yep," he said, staring at her. "Sure does."

He didn't think Jess would blush over such an easy compliment, but color rose to her cheeks, and she blinked and wiggled in her seat. He liked flustering her.

"Hey, you two." A familiar voice sounded from the shadows, and Dylan McKay's smug face came into view. "I hope you don't mind me coming over to say hello. Saw the two of you dancing a minute ago. Didn't have the balls to cut in, Zane. Excuse my language, Jessica, but the two of you looked hot and heavy out there. And Zane, it's good to see you without those crutches."

"Hi, Dylan," she said with enough damn cheerfulness for both of them.

"Hey, you," he said, giving Jess a wink.

Zane kept a smile plastered on his face. He liked Dylan, but damn his keen perception and his untimely interruption. "Dylan."

"So, how do you like this place?" the actor asked.

"Very much," Jess said.

"We were just about to dive into our meal." Zane picked up his fork.

"Yeah, the food's pretty good here. And you can't beat…"

Lights flashed, and cameras snapped, one, two, three clicks a second. Zane caught sight of a trio of paparazzi, kneeling down, angling cameras and snapping pictures of Dylan. Damn it.

Dylan turned, giving them a charming smile as Zane wrangled Jess into his arms, turning away from the cameras. Shielding Jess, his first instinct was to protect her from the intrusive photographers. He hated paparazzi ambushes. But Dylan didn't seem fazed. He posed for a few shots, and then the manager rushed over, shooing the photographers away from his customers.

"So sorry, Mr. McKay. This usually doesn't happen."

"I know, Jeffrey. It's okay. It must be a slow news day. I'm here with some buddies. No hot chicks on my arm tonight."

The manager didn't smile at Dylan's attempt at humor. He took his job seriously. "I apologize to you as well, Mr. Williams," he said.

"No harm done." He had to be gracious. The manager couldn't have prevented this from happening. It happened all the time in every place imaginable, especially to Dylan.

The guy was a walking magnet for the tabloids. He seemed to love the attention.

After the manager walked off, Dylan shrugged. "What can I say? I'm sorry. This place used to be off their radar."

"It's not your fault," Jess was quick to say. "Like Zane said, no harm done."

Dylan stared at Jess for a moment, his eyes smiling, and then focused on Zane. "It's good to see you two together like this."

Like what? Zane was tempted to ask. Instead, he sent him his best mind-your-business look.

"O…kay," Dylan said. "Well, I'll be getting back to my friends now. Have a nice evening. Oh, and Jess, I'll see you on the beach."

Jess smiled.

"Bye, Dylan," Zane said, and the guy walked off. If only Dylan's flirty relationship with Jessica didn't grate so much on his nerves.

She touched his arm. "Are you angry?"

Dylan pissed him off, but that's not what she meant. "No. But I don't like having our time together interrupted like that. You don't need to be exposed to my real world. It's bad enough I have to deal with it."

"It's okay." Her face went gooey soft. "It wasn't so bad."

They'd never set boundaries or labeled what was happening between them, except to say she was on the rebound and he was the guy enjoying the privilege. But he wanted to spend every minute with her while she was here. She would go home soon. And he'd have to deal with it. She was forbidden fruit, and at times, his conscience warred with his desire for her. She was vulnerable right now and had come to live with him to heal her wounds. The last thing he wanted was to add to her pain. He'd never knowingly take advantage of her, but was he leading her on or helping her heal? He had to think it was healing for them to be together.

Right now, things were simple, but when the time came for her to return home, he'd have to let her go.

Her palm caressed his cheek. The touch was gentle, caring, and her eyes simmered with enough warmth to light a fire. When she leaned in and kissed him, something snapped in his heart. He wouldn't name it, didn't want to think about it. The sensations roiling in his gut scared the stuffing out of him. The mistake he'd made had cost his wife her life, and he wasn't going back there again. Falling in love was already checked off his bucket list.

Leaning back in his seat, he gave her a smile. "Our food's getting cold, sweetheart."

She blinked, and the heat in her eyes evaporated.

He hated disappointing her, but he had nothing else to say on the subject.

Jessica loved working for Zane. It gave her a sense of purpose, and she enjoyed gaining a new perspective on life. As a grade-school teacher, her world revolved around children, shaping and molding them into good students and eager learners. But this work had its own rewards. This morning she'd already spoken to Zane's fan club president, made a list of devotees she needed to send autographed photos to, and spoken with Mrs. Elise Woolery, a senior citizen who wrote to Zane every month. Yes, at the age of eighty-four, the woman was a Zane Zealot. She was his Super Fan. Mariah had made a special point to make sure Zane read and answered this woman's letters. Jessica would do no less.

Sitting at the office desk, she was reading her heart-warming letter when her cell phone rang. She glanced at the screen and smiled before answering. "Hi, Mama."

"Hi, honey."

"Is something wrong? Your voice…"

"Honey, I'm fine. It's not that, but how are you?"

She was flying high, happy as a clam, strolling on Moonlight Beach shores and spending time with Zane. Last night had been incredible. Except for the crazy camera goons coming out of the woodwork and some odd moments afterward, it had been a picture-perfect day and night. Riding at Ruby Ranch, dinner, dancing and making love with Zane afterward was up there on her Top Ten List of Best Days. What more could a girl ask for?

A lot, a voice in her head screamed.

She ignored it.

"I'm fine, Mom. What is it? Did Steven make another stupid move? Is Judy pregnant or something? I'm telling you right now I'm over it, whatever it is."

"No, honey. I haven't heard anything more about Steven. It's just that…well, have you read the *Daily Inquiry* this morning?"

"Mama, you know I don't read that stuff. And neither do you. What's this all about?"

"I mean, I was sort of used to it with Janie. Zane protected her mostly, and the press loved them. But you, honey. Well, there's a picture of you and Zane, and it's quite shocking."

"There's a picture of me and Zane?"

"On the front page. My neighbor Esther showed it to me this morning. And after that, my phone hasn't stopped ringing."

"It hasn't?" It was noon in Texas. Damn those photographers. She'd thought they were only after Dylan. She should've known better, not that she had any way of stopping the invasion of privacy. "Mama, it's nothing, really. You know the life Zane leads. We were dining out and were ambushed by the Hollywood nut jobs. That's all."

"You changed your hair. You're blonde now. And the dress you were wearing…well, it was quite revealing. Zane had you in his arms, baby girl, and it looked to me as if—"

"He was protecting me from the cameras, that's all."

"Is that *all*, honey?"

She nibbled her lip. What could she say to her mother?

That she'd been sleeping with Zane and they'd been helping each other come to terms with their own personal demons? Could she honestly tell her mother that? No. Her mother would worry like crazy. She didn't know that the new and improved Jessica could handle anything that came her way. God, she only hoped she wasn't wrong about that.

"Jessica, that picture of you…well, do you know how much you look like Janie now?"

Something powerful stung her heart. The subtle implication wasn't anything she hadn't already thought of a hundred times in her head. Was that the attraction Zane had to her? She looked enough like Janie for him to gravitate her way.

"I don't want you to get hurt again."

"I know, Mama. I don't plan to."

Swinging her chair toward the computer, she keyed into the *Daily Inquiry* site on the internet. The front-page picture came up, and there she was, her neckline plunging and Zane's arms around her shoulders possessively, his body half covering hers in a proprietary way. But the headline was what grabbed her the most. "Zane Williams Dating Wife Look-alike." The subtitle wasn't much better. "Who Is His Mystery Love?"

"Holy moly, Mama. I just looked it up." Good thing the paparazzi didn't do much investigating. She could only imagine the headline if they knew she was Janie's younger sister.

"See what I mean?"

"I do. But this will pass. Tomorrow someone else will be their fodder."

"I know that. I'm not worried about the picture or the headline. I'm only worried about you and what you're feeling right now."

"Mama, just know I'm happy. Zane has been incredible, and I'm making friends, enjoying the work I'm doing here."

"Is Zane there now?"

"No, he's having physical therapy." She gasped as a

thought struck her. "Mama, you're not going to call him about this, are you?"

Her mother paused long enough to worry her. "Mother?"

"No, not if you don't want me to."

"I definitely don't want you to. Promise me you won't."

Gosh, the last thing she needed was her mother intervening in her love life. She was the one who had insisted Jessica come here. The damage was already done. Her mama could only make things worse. She hung up on a cheery note, convincing her mother she was fine, and resumed her work.

An hour later, she heard Zane's car pull up. Giddiness stirred inside her, and her heart warmed. She was becoming a lovesick puppy dog where he was concerned. She heard him enter the house, and his footsteps grew louder on the slate flooring as he approached. Seconds later, he was standing in front of her, a newspaper in his hand. He tossed it onto the desk, and she gave it a glance. "Sorry, sweetheart. I've got my manager doing some repair on this. Ideally, he can keep your name out of it." He studied her a second. "You don't look surprised."

"Oh, I was very surprised when my mama called to tell me about it," she said softly.

"Your mama saw this?" he nearly shrieked.

She nodded. "Just about all of Beckon has seen it by now."

He ran a hand down his face, pulling his skin tight. "Oh, man."

"Zane? What are you worried about?" Looking into his pained eyes frightened her.

He came around the desk and, taking her arms, pulled her up against him. "You. I'm worried about you," his said softly into her ear. He tucked her into an embrace while his breath warmed her skin and her spine got all tingly.

"Don't. I'm okay."

"Your mama must think I'm a jerk, subjecting you to this.

You have to go back to Beckon one day. I don't want it to be harder on you than it has to be. I'm so sorry, sweetheart."

You have to go back to Beckon one day.

He was right, she would have to return to her hometown one day. Her mind rebelled at the thought. He kissed her again and eased the battle going on inside her head. Oh, boy.

She gazed at him and was floored by the genuine look of concern on his face.

"How was your appointment?"

He pulled away from her and shrugged. "Fine. I don't think I needed it, but—"

"You need it. So you did okay. It wasn't too hard?"

"I've been swimming, riding and dancing on this foot. Seems I'm doing my own rehab."

"You're lucky you haven't reinjured yourself, babe."

He grinned.

"It's not funny."

"I'm not laughing at that. I like it when you call me 'babe.'"

"Well, if you like that, I have an idea I think you might enjoy."

"Does it involve a bed and soft sheets?"

"No, it involves being poolside with some beautiful hot chicks."

One week later, at the Ventura Women's Senior Center, an hour's ride from Moonlight Beach, Jessica sat poolside in the audience of geriatric hot chicks. The scent of chorine was heavy in the air of the enclosed pool area that opened into the center's recreation center. Zane had his butt in a chair, facing his eager fans with guitar in hand—he'd been brushing up at home—and it sounded to her as if he hadn't lost his touch. Playing guitar was probably like riding a bicycle. Once you mastered it, you never forgot.

Zane's Super Fan Elise Woolery, was all smiles today. She sat in the front row next to her friends, all of whom she'd coaxed into becoming great fans of Zane's, as well. As smokin' hot as Zane appeared to his younger audience, he had the wholesome good looks and Southern charm that any of these women would admire in a son.

Zane had balked at the idea of coming here, not because he wasn't charitable. Nothing was further from the truth. But he didn't know if he had the chops or the will to get back onstage and entertain the masses anymore. It had taken only one little ole note from Elise, saying she'd had a bad week physically, her arthritis so painful she couldn't get out of bed in the mornings, and listening to Zane's songs had helped her get by. That letter and Jessica's urgings had convinced him to play this private concert. He insisted on no press, and Jessica agreed. This wasn't a photo op. It wasn't done for his public image, either. He'd agreed because basically he'd been humbled by her letter and wanted to help.

Zane faced his audience. "Well, now. It's nice to be in such fine company. I guess you all are stuck with me for the next hour or two, so let's start things off." He nodded for Jessica to bring Elise up front and center. There was an empty chair beside him.

"Elise?" She helped the woman sit down next to him. The older woman waved her hand over her chest as the silvery-blue in her eyes gleamed.

"How are you this afternoon?" he asked.

Giddy as a school girl, she nodded and spoke softly. "I'm just fine."

"Yes, you are," Zane said. "Ready for a song?"

She gazed out at the envious women in the audience, her friends in the front fidgeting in their seats, too excited to sit still.

"I am, Mr. Williams."

"Zane," he corrected her, taking her hand. "May I call you Elise?"

"Oh, my, yes."

Zane performed for over an hour, and he'd never sounded

better. Just Zane and his guitar, without all the usual fanfare, lights or band to back him up. His voice was clear and honest and mesmerizing.

After the performance, one by one the seniors said their goodbyes and thanked him, often offering kisses on the cheek before leaving the facility. Elise stayed until the end and chatted with Zane. Jessica didn't contribute much to the conversation. It seemed as though through her letters, Elise and Zane knew each other pretty well, but Jessica did take a number of photos, promising Elise she'd send them to her home address as soon as she could.

"You can thank Jessica here for arranging this," Zane was saying.

"Thank you, Jessica. This made my whole year. I swear today, my arthritis just vanished. I think I'll go home, put on one of Zane's records and dance a jig."

And later, sitting in the backseat of a limo, Zane reached for Jessica's hand as they headed down the highway. He didn't say much as he stared out the window, and every once in a while, he'd give her hand a squeeze.

If she could put a name on this sense of peace and total belonging, she'd call it bliss.

The sea glistened in the moonlight, calm tonight, the placid waves grazing the shore. It was a night like many she'd shared with Zane these past weeks, walking the shore in the dark, holding hands, enjoying the beach after the locals went home.

"You're quiet tonight," Zane said as they strolled along.

She wasn't a complainer. She didn't want to mar the perfection they'd seemed to achieve lately.

"I think I ate something that didn't agree with me."

Zane squeezed her hand lightly. "We can head back. We're only half a mile from the house."

"No, it's okay. The fresh air is doing me good."

"You sure?"

"I'm sure."

"'Cause you know, now that my rehab is done, I could pick you up and carry you all the way."

She chuckled, and the movement caused her stomach to curl. "Oh."

She wanted desperately to put her hand to her belly, but she didn't want to draw his attention there. They were having such a wonderful evening. She managed a small smile instead. "That won't be necessary."

"Could be fun."

"I don't doubt it. You'd probably dunk me into the ocean first or deliver me into your shower, like you did the other night."

"And you enjoyed every second. But I wouldn't do that to you tonight, sweetheart. I can see on your face that you're exhausted." He pivoted, taking her with him. "C'mon. You should get to bed."

"Okay, maybe you're right."

She didn't have the strength to argue with him. Zane had a charity event at the children's hospital in the city tomorrow, and she didn't want to miss it. It wasn't an extravaganza by any means, just an artist making the rounds and singing songs with the kids She hadn't had any difficulty convincing Zane to do it. When it came to making children feel better, Zane was all in.

"Excuse me? You said I was right about something?"

"Very funny." Gosh, her voice sounded suddenly weak. Whatever strength she had left seemed to seep right out of her. Her limbs lost all their juice. "Zane, I'm, uh, really tired." A wave of fatigue stopped her steps in the sand.

Zane halted and gave her a quick once-over, his eyes dark with concern. He lifted her effortlessly, and she wound her arms around his neck. "I've got you. Hang on, honey."

"I don't know what hit me all of a sudden."

"Just rest against me and close your eyes. I'll have you home in no time."

And minutes later, they entered the house. She insisted Zane deposit her in her own bedroom. He balked at first. He said he wanted to keep an eye on her tonight. "Are you sure?"

She needed a place to crash. And if she had a bug or the flu, she could be contagious. Zane didn't need to get sick on her account. "I'm sure. Thanks for the lift." Literally. She smiled, and his eyes grew sympathetic in response.

"Anytime."

"I just need to sleep this off."

"Can I help you get ready for bed?" he asked.

"I'll manage, Zane. Thanks for the thought."

"Okay if I come in to check on you later? I won't wake you."

She could see it meant a lot to him by the protective look in his eyes. "Yes, I'd like that."

"If you need anything during the night, just call for me."

When she'd had the flu during spring break last year, Steven hadn't so much as offered to bring her a bowl of soup. He'd told her he'd keep his distance so she could rest up and get better. He couldn't afford to get sick. She'd received a total of one phone call from him during her recuperation. What a fool she'd been. The signs were all there, but she'd refused to see them.

"Thank you, Zane."

He smiled, but the worry in his eyes touched her deeply. "Good night, sweet Jess." He placed a kiss on her forehead, tossed the sheets back on the bed and gave her a lingering smile before he walked out of the room and closed the door.

Her hands trembled as she put on her nightie and tucked herself into bed. She hadn't lasted but a minute when her belly rattled and the turmoil reached up into her throat, gagging her. Her stomach recoiled, and she covered her mouth, clamping it shut as she raced to the toilet.

It wasn't a pretty sight, but she emptied her stomach in just about thirty seconds.

Sitting back on the floor, she closed her eyes and took big breaths of air in order to calm her stomach. Whatever it was, she hoped it was gone.

Bye. Bye.

Arrivederci.

Good riddance.

She rose slowly and leaned against the marble counter. One look at her chalky face in the mirror told her to wash up and get her butt back into bed. She splashed water on her cheeks, chin, throat and arms, cooling and cleansing herself, and then headed back to bed on wobbly jelly legs. Her eyes closed to the distant serenade of Zane's beautiful voice coming from downstairs as he rehearsed his music for tomorrow's event.

In the morning, her weakened body felt bulldozed. Her head was propped by the pillow and her limbs lay flaccid on the bed as she absorbed the comfort of the luxurious mattress. She missed having Zane's arms around her, but she needed these hours of privacy to rest up.

A soft knock at her door snapped her eyes open. "Jess, are you awake?"

She sat taller in the bed, ran her fingers through her hair and pinched her cheeks, hoping she still didn't look like death warmed over. "Yes, come in."

Zane entered the room, assessing her from top to bottom, and took a seat on the side of the bed. "Morning. Are you feeling any better today?"

"Yes. Just a little tired still. But I'm sure once I get up and eat something, I'll perk right up."

He looked like a zillion bucks. Dressed in crisp new jeans, his signature sterling silver Z belt buckle and a Western shirt the color of sea coral decorated tastefully with rhinestones that outlined a horse and rider, Zane resembled the superstar that he was. His concert shirts were custom-made by a trusty tailor, and this one was perfect for a day with children. "Glad to hear it. Mrs. Lopez has breakfast ready whenever you are."

The mention of food riled her stomach. And blood drained from her face. Her eyes drifted toward the digital clock inside a wall unit near her bed. It was almost ten! "Zane! I had no idea how late I slept. Give me a few minutes to get dressed and I'll—"

As she hinged her body forward, Zane's arms were on her shoulders, pressing her back down. "Whoa, Jess. Slow down."

Dizziness followed her as her head hit the pillow. The world spun for a second, and when it stopped, a soft sigh escaped her. "But I'm supposed to go with you today." It was her job, her duty as Zane's personal assistant. Zane wasn't used to making appearances on his own. He always had an assistant to usher him through the process.

"I didn't have the heart to wake you. I'm leaving in just a few minutes. What I want you to do is take the day off and relax. I'll be back in a few hours."

"I don't want to miss it."

He took hold of her hand. "I wish you could come, too."

"I'm sorry."

"Don't be. I'm sorry you're not feeling well."

"I'll be sure to call Mrs. Russo this morning. She's in charge at Children's Hospital, and I made all the arrangements through her. I'll tell her the situation."

"Don't go to any trouble. I'm sure I'll be fine."

"No trouble." She picked up her cell phone. "I've got the number right here."

Zane's gaze swept over her rumpled sheets and the spot where she'd conjured up her phone. "You sleep with your cell phone?" His incredulous voice tickled the funny bone inside her head.

"When I'm not sleeping with you."

He grinned and kissed the top of her head. "Feel better."

"Thanks."

As soon as Zane left, she made the call and was relieved that Mrs. Russo was amenable to sticking by Zane's side today, keeping him on schedule. She was a fan and was looking forward to the day, as well. Jessica hung up, convinced Zane would enjoy himself, doing what he loved to do. He'd be fine on his own. He liked being around children. Singing to them and with them would be second nature to a guy who'd lived and breathed country music as a boy.

A short time later, ringing blasted in her ear, and she lifted her eyelids. When had she drifted off? How long had she been in sleep land? She squinted to ward off the sunshine blazing into her window. The last thing she remembered was speaking with the director at the hospital regarding Zane's appearance. She took a few seconds to awaken fully, blinking and stretching. Gosh, she felt better, her stomach didn't ache and her head cleared of all the fuzz.

All systems go.

She grabbed her phone and greeted her caller on the third ring. "Hello, Mariah. It's good to hear from you."

Mariah had been calling in at least once a week to make sure things were going smoothly for her and checking in on Zane. Jessica appreciated her diligence and thoughtfulness, but she'd already spoken with Mariah earlier in the week. "Is everything alright?"

"Everything is actually better than I hoped." Enthusiasm that had been vacant in Mariah's voice since her mother's ordeal was making a sparkling comeback. "The last time I spoke with Zane, I told him my mother was being re-evaluated by the doctors. Well, the good news is that even though Mom has something of a long road ahead of her, she's recovered enough to come home from the transitional facility. My sister plans on taking over from now on. She'll have the help of a caregiver during the week. And I'll come home on the weekends whenever I can to help out. I tried to reach Zane to tell him I'll be coming back to work starting Monday morning, but I think he shut his phone off."

Mariah was coming back in five days? The news pounded Jessica's skull. Five days. She'd known this day would come, but she'd been too busy living in the moment to worry about it. "Oh, uh…yes. He's not here. He's doing a show at the children's hospital."

"That's where he really shines," Mariah was saying. "Anyway, you don't have to pinch-hit for me anymore. You, my savior, are off the hook."

She was off the hook? But she liked being on the hook. She *was* hooked on Zane.

Wow. Just like that, her life was about to change again. Mariah would return to work, and things would go back to the status quo. No more sunset dinners with Zane or moonlit strolls or making love on his big bed during the night. The happy place in her heart deflated. Like when the air inside a balloon was released, she fizzled.

"I'm happy to hear your mother's doing well, Mariah." She really was. It was good news, and she focused on that and what Mariah had gone through to get to this point. "And I'll be sure to tell Zane."

"Thanks, hon. I know you've done a great job in my absence. Zane sings your praises and tells me not to worry about a thing."

"Well, there wasn't all that much to do." Except to fall for the boss. "And you left impeccable notes."

"It's a flaw of mine. I'm a detail person. Makes most people crazy, but it comes in handy for the kind of work that I do. I'm happy Zane had you these past weeks. And I'm eager to come back to work. What about you, Jessica? How's your summer going?"

The summer was more than half-over. If she stayed, nothing would be the same. She wouldn't be working alongside Zane, and she couldn't very well carry on with him right under Mariah's nose. She had no name for her relationship with Zane. She wasn't his girlfriend. He hadn't made a commitment to her in any way. Did he look at her as a forbidden fling? He wanted to be her rebound guy, and he'd accomplished that and more. He got an A for effort.

"My coming back doesn't mean you have to leave, you know. Please don't on my account," Mariah was saying. But in fact, her coming back meant that very thing. Zane hadn't spoken about the future with Jessica. He wasn't one to plan anymore. He took things as they came now. Hadn't he encouraged her to do the same? "I would love to get to know you better."

"I feel the same way, Mariah. But unfortunately, I can't promise you that. I...should be getting home soon. There are things I have to do."

Prepare her lesson plans for the new school year.

Avoid Steven at all costs.

Fall back in step with single life in Beckon.

Try not to think about Zane.

"I understand. When home is calling, you must go."

"When Beckon beckons."

Mariah chuckled.

"Sorry. It's a dumb joke the locals think is clever. Small-town humor."

"Sounds kinda sweet. Will you tell Zane I'm sorry I missed him? It was nice talking to you, Jess."

"Sure, I'll tell Zane as soon as he gets back, and same here. Good talking to you."

Bittersweet emotions snagged her heart. She was thankful Mariah's mother was on the mend, but the thought of leaving Zane to return to Beckon was killing her. He'd be home soon.

And she'd have to tell him the news.

Ten

"You're staying," Zane said resolutely. His handsome face was inches from hers as she lay on a beach blanket on the sand right outside his back door, her head propped by a towel. She'd needed some sun to put color on her sickly cheeks while she tried to figure out where in heck her life was headed.

"How can you say that so easily?"

He'd plopped down beside her just minutes ago, wearing shorts and an aqua Hawaiian shirt. He'd been in a good mood since coming back from the children's hospital, and she'd had to spoil it by giving him the news that she'd be returning home.

"It is easy. You're my summer guest. What's so hard about that?"

He made it seem so simple, and he'd brought along his arsenal of secret weapons to convince her. His ripped chest grazed her breasts, teasing and tormenting her. Powerful arms braced on either side of her head surrounded her with strength, and that amazing mouth of his hovered so close she could almost taste it. His presence surrounded her, sucking oxygen from her rational brain.

"It'll be awkward. These past weeks it's been just us, and now that Mariah will be here most of the time, it won't be the same. She'll guess what's going on."

As he cupped her head with both hands, she had nowhere

to look but deep into his eyes. "She probably already knows, Jess. Mariah keeps up on everything, and I'm sure she's seen that tabloid photo of us. But if it makes you feel any better, I'll be up-front with her and explain the situation." Zane lowered his head and brushed his lips over hers. "It won't matter if she knows, as long as you stay."

Yes, yes. His kiss was a potent persuader. Oh, how she wanted to agree with him. She shouldn't care what people thought. But darn it, she did, and her heart was at stake, too. "I'm not... I don't do... Never mind."

"Jess," he said softly, his finger outlining the lips he'd just kissed. His touch seeped into her skin as he curved his fingertips around and around the rim of her mouth as if he'd never touched anything so fascinating. She'd hoped he'd ask her to stay, but she wanted more. She wanted the happily-ever-after that wasn't bound to happen.

He claimed her lips and took her into another world. When he was through kissing her, his deep, dark eyes were hot, heavy and filled with desire. "You can't go yet. This is new and real, and right now I can't offer you more than that." His words were raw with emotion. "But I'm asking you to stay."

New and real? Those were promising words. Hope began to build in her, but she warned herself not to be a fool. She couldn't get blindsided again. She had to face the truth head-on. She didn't know if Zane had the capacity to love again. He was and always would be devoted to her sister. Could she live with that? Could she spend the next five weeks with him and enjoy herself? The new Jess said yes. *Go for it, you idiot!* But the old Jess buried deep down wasn't quite so fearless, and she rose up occasionally to plant dire warnings in her ear. "I want to...but—"

"Sweetheart, you don't have to make up your mind right this minute. Take time to think it over."

Her shoulders relaxed as she blew breath from her lungs. "Okay, I can do that," she said softly.

"Good." He rose and offered her his hand.

"Where are we going?"

"One guess." He waggled his brows. He was six feet two inches of gorgeous, rugged, tan and aroused.

"You don't play fair, Zane Williams."

"*You* don't play fair. That bikini does things to my head and…" He looked down past his waistband. "If I don't get inside soon, I'll be arrested for indecent exposure."

She took his hand, and he yanked her up. She fell against him, her hands landing on his broad, bronzed chest. He smelled of sunshine and sand and sunscreen, and at this moment, she couldn't imagine not being with him.

"What would the residents of the Ventura Women's Senior Center say to that?"

A smile spread wide across his face. "They'd probably invite me back with an engraved invitation."

She laughed along with him, and her day brightened.

Jessica gave her body and soul to Zane, and the past three days had been magical. They rode horses, had moonlight swims, dined and danced together. Zane took her to the new restaurant, and they'd surveyed the progress, sharing ideas. He helped her answer fan mail, giving attention to questions and signing the letters personally. At night their lovemaking was intense, the heat level rising above anything she'd ever experienced before, but it was more than that. Emotions were involved now, their time together precious. Each night before they drifted off to sleep, Zane would hold her close and whisper in her ear, "Stay." In the morning, they'd rise at the crack of dawn to walk along the beach before the world woke up.

Except for a growing suspicion she might be pregnant, everything was perfect.

The idea of carrying Zane's baby made her glow inside, the beaming light of hope strong. It wasn't an ideal situation, but how could she not embrace the new life she might be carrying? She'd been queasy in the mornings ever since her bout of illness, but she managed to hide it from Zane for the most part. She ate little in the mornings, to his raised eyebrows, claiming she put on weight fast and needed to be disciplined. "You haven't got an ounce of fat on you," he'd said.

"And I want to keep it that way." Not entirely true. She wasn't a big believer in stick-thin female bodies, especially since she might be described as voluptuous. But most men bought that explanation, and for now, feminine vanity was a white lie that was necessary.

She'd been overly tired, too, but when Zane noticed, she attributed her fatigue to the energetic pace they'd been keeping in and out of bed. And she was overdue on her monthly cycle.

Locked inside her bathroom, she held the pregnancy test in her hand, waiting those precious few minutes that might change the course of her life. Zane was out shopping—which was bizarre since the man would rather break his other foot than step into a store—and she would use this time alone to deal with whatever came her way. Admittedly, it had taken her half an hour to muster the courage to break open the package and pee on the stick. And now that she had, her pulse pounded in anticipation.

Seconds ticked by, and then she glanced down and got the news.

She leaned against the sink and pressed her eyelids closed.

"Okay." She took a breath.

The new Jess was strong. She could do this.

Tears stung behind her eyes.

"Jess?"

Oh, no. Zane was home. What was he doing back so soon?

"I'll just be a minute." Her voice wobbled from behind the bathroom door.

"Okay, mind if I wait for you in here?"

"Uh, no. It's okay." Shaking, she scrambled to toss all signs of the pregnancy test away. She wrapped everything in toilet paper and shoved it into the bottom of her trash container. She took another few seconds to wash her face and straighten herself out mentally. Then she opened the door.

Zane was lying across her bed, staring out the window. He sat up the minute he saw her and smiled, a winning, charming, loving smile that seared straight into her heart.

"Everything okay, sweetheart?"

She nodded and bit her lip to keep herself from saying more.

Zane studied her face. Did he see the truth in her expression? She lowered her eyes, and that's when she saw a small, square, sapphire-blue velvet box on the spot next to him.

"Sit with me?" He picked up the box and patted that same spot for her to take a seat.

She did and turned his way. He had something to say, and she was all ears.

"Recently, you gave me a gift that was especially meaningful. And now, it's my turn to give you something. Not in reciprocation but because, well, you deserve this. I had this made for you."

His eyes contained a genuine spark of excitement as he placed the box in her hand. Whatever it was, Zane was eager for her to see it. She didn't make him wait. Gently she opened the lid and lifted out a unique charm bracelet. She'd never seen one made with diamonds before. "Oh, Zane." She was truly swept away. "This is…" A lump in her throat blocked her next words. She was speechless.

The silver-and-diamond bracelet held three charms and glittered brightly enough to light all of Moonlight Beach. The charms were well thought-out and special to the person that she was. The first charm was a teacher's apple that reminded her of her students, the second was a schoolbook with opened pages and the third was a pair of eyeglasses, which, up until a few weeks ago, were her mainstay. Every charm was exquisitely outlined by small diamonds. A tiny heart hung from the clasp, engraved with one word in italic script: *Stay.*

"Let me try it on you," Zane said, and she put out her hand.

"Thank you," she said finally. She couldn't have been more surprised. Zane fastened the clasp around her wrist. The fit was perfect, and there was something about a personalized gift, no matter what it was, that made her feel cared for. There were no words to express how meaningful this gift was to her. Zane had outdone himself. "It's very special."

"Just like you. I'm glad you like it," he said.

"I do. You don't play fair, Zane." It was getting to be his signature move. Make her want him even more than she already did.

"I swear to you, I had this bracelet ordered weeks ago, and then, well, the heart was just added on this week. You can't fault a guy for trying."

She put her hand to his cheek and gazed into his eyes. "That's sweet." And then she kissed him, quickly and passionately, before she pulled away, her heart in her throat.

She loved this man with all of her heart.

And she *wasn't* carrying his child.

Sadness blanketed her body, a shallow sliver of sorrow of what wasn't to be.

"Are you sure you're okay, Jess?" Zane studied her movements as she approached his bed. He lifted his sheets and welcomed her. He wanted her with him tonight, sex or no sex. She was special to him, and he didn't want to press her if she needed more rest.

After he returned to the house today, he couldn't wait to see her. His gift was burning a hole in his pocket, so he'd waited for her on her bed. When she'd stepped out of the bathroom and he'd looked at her, he'd seen a haunted expression on her face, and she'd been overly quiet. He worried over her health, but he sensed it was something more than her having an upset stomach. She'd looked sad, and a transparent sheen of despair seemed to cover her eyes.

She'd liked the gift—he could tell that much—and that brightened her mood, but her eyes never really returned to the Jess sparkle he was used to. She'd kept the bracelet on during the day, and there were moments when he'd catch her touching the links, tracing her fingertips over the charms tenderly. After what she'd been through this year, if the gift told her she was appreciated, she was worthy of beautiful things and she was desirable as a woman, then mission accomplished. Zane wanted her to feel all of those things. He'd wanted her to know what she had come to mean to him.

"I'm feeling better tonight," she said. She climbed in and scooted close to him. His arms tightened around her automatically, and he rolled so that her back was up against his chest.

Like it or not, Mae Holcomb put him in charge of her daughter. His first responsibility was to see to her health. Precious little else mattered. He'd failed where Janie was concerned, and he certainly wasn't going to let something happen to Jess while she was here with him. Not on his watch.

"Glad to hear it."

She still looked weary, as if a burden weighed her down. Was she deliberating about staying with him for the rest of the summer? Right now, breathing in the sweet scent of her hair and having her body cuddled up against him, he couldn't imagine her leaving in two days, but he wouldn't pressure her. She needed to come to the conclusion that they were good together, on her own. He'd done everything he could do, short of begging, to convince her to stay, but ultimately it was her decision.

Pushing silken strands away from her face, he kissed her earlobe. "If you need to sleep, I can just hold you tonight, babe. Or…"

She turned around in his arms, her features softening and her eyes tender and liquid. "Or," she said. "Definitely or."

Zane made slow, easy love to her, and she fell in sync with his body movements. He savored every inch of her with gentle strokes and touches. And she did the same to him. He loved the feel of her hands on him, exploring, probing and possessing him in small doses. Little by little, hour by hour, minute by minute, Jess was filling his life.

He cared about her. Worried when she was sick. Praised her accomplishments. Was impressed by her feisty spirit. Wanted to see her happy.

She mattered to him.

And after the explosion that burst before his eyes in warm colors, Jessica's sighs of contentment, completion and satisfaction settled peacefully in his heart. He never remembered being so in tune with another person before. *Except with Janie.*

A wave of guilt blindsided him. Up until now, he'd been able to separate the two, but was he disparaging his deceased wife's memory by finding comfort and some joy with her sister? Was he hurting Jessica and dishonoring his wife?

Zane carefully removed himself from a sleeping Jess and padded away from the bed. Words he hadn't found before came rushing forth, pounding inside his head. He had a song to finish, and the lyrics blasted in his ears now. The song that had haunted him for months would finally see the light of day.

Jessica just put on the finishing touches on her makeup, a hint of pale-green eye shadow and toner under her eyes to conceal the dark shadows from the ungodly remnants of whatever bug she'd had. Her appetite was coming back, thankfully, and she put on a lemon-yellow sundress decorated with tiny white daisies to make her feel human again. She looked at her reflection in the mirror. The dress did the trick. She had a dash of color in her face now, and wearing something fun perked up her spirits.

As she walked into the kitchen, Mrs. Lopez was just setting out her morning meal.

"Thank you," she said, taking a seat. She could definitely handle hard-boiled eggs, toast and a cup of tea. "You always know exactly what I want to eat. How do you do that?"

"I am like a little mouse, observing, watching. I can see you are feeling better, but the stomach needs time to rest. Today, you eat a little. Tomorrow, a little bit more. If you want something more, you just need to tell me."

"No, no. This is perfect. Exactly what I feel like having. It's…late."

"*Sí*. You've been waking late."

"The bug I had wore me out."

Minutes later, just as she was finishing up her last bite of toast and sip of tea, a knock on the deck door brought her head up.

Mrs. Lopez was there before Jessica pushed her chair out to rise. "Hello, Mr. McKay," she said politely, her olive face blossoming. Even Zane's housekeeper was starstruck. Dylan McKay had the same effect on all women, young and old, happily married or not.

"Hello, Mrs. Lopez. I took a walk down the beach to see if Zane could spare a few minutes for me this morning."

"He is not here."

"But I am." Jessica walked over to the door. "Dylan, hi! Is there something I can help you with?"

Dylan had a briefcase tucked under his arm, yet dressed in plaid board shorts and a teal-blue muscle shirt, he looked like a walking advertisement for sunscreen or surfboards. Hardly businessman attire, but that was Dylan.

"Hey, Jess."

"Thanks, Mrs. Lopez," she said, and the woman backed away.

"What's up?"

He brushed past her and stepped into the kitchen. "Looking beautiful as always," Dylan said. It wasn't a line with Dylan. He had a genuine appreciation for women, and he seemed to love to compliment them.

"You're looking fit yourself," she said. "Still running?"

He scrunched up his face. "Yeah. It's getting old."

"Why don't you break it up? Do five miles in the morning, five miles at night?"

His brows rose. "Wow, smart and beautiful. Does Zane know what a treasure you are?"

"I don't know. Why don't you ask him?" She grinned.

"Well, I like your idea, Little Miss Smarty Pants. I might just try breaking up the run and see how it goes."

Mrs. Lopez stood by the oven with a coffee pot in hand, reminding Jess of her manners.

"Would you like a cup of coffee? Water? Juice? Anything?" How comfortable she felt in the role of hostess to Zane's friends. It was something she didn't want to end.

"No, thanks. I'm good right now. Actually, I brought a revised script for Zane to look over. The screenwriter made some adjustments that I think really enhance the story. I've highlighted the parts that would affect Zane. Would you like to see them?"

"Of course!" It sounded better than watching her nails dry, and she was still on the clock as far as work went, even if it was Saturday. "I'd love to. Why don't you come into the office?".

He followed her, and as she entered the office, she went to the wood shutters first, opening them and allowing eastern light to enter the room. "Have a seat."

"Wow, looks like Zane's doing some writing."

Dylan was eyeing Zane's desk littered with sheet music

crumpled into tight balls. Ready to clear away the mess, she noticed the waste basket was full to the brim with the same. Mrs. Lopez worked her way through the rooms every morning. It was evident she hadn't made it to this room yet. "Yeah, I guess he is."

"That's good, right? As far as I know, he hasn't written a song for years."

Since Janie's death.

"I suppose so."

Dylan sat down on the sofa and opened his portfolio. "Do you know where he keeps the original script I gave him? We can compare the two. I'm eager to see if you think the changes work as well as I do."

"Sure. I think Zane locked it up in his desk for safekeeping. Just give me a second to get the key."

"No problem. I'm a patient man."

She doubted that. She moved quickly to retrieve the key from a set Zane kept in his bedroom dresser drawer. She came back to find Dylan with head down, making notes on the script. "Okay, here we go."

She unlocked the bottom drawer, and sure enough, there was the script. She made a grab for it and did a rapid double take at the folder that lay beneath it. In black lettering and handwritten by Zane, the title was spelled out. "Janie's Song. Final."

Zane never mentioned he was writing a song about Janie.

All that sheet music? She had to guess that Zane had been working on this recently. As recently as last night, maybe? She'd woken in the middle of the night and opened her eyes to an empty pillow beside her. She'd heard distant strumming and figured Zane was practicing his guitar again. She thought nothing of it and had fallen right back to sleep. But now, as she glanced at all the rejected papers strewn across his desk and bubbling up from his trash, she knew it had to be true.

It was and always had been all about Janie.

How could she be jealous of her dead sister?

Tears welled in her eyes. She felt sick to her stomach again.

She handed Dylan the first version of the script and went back to the drawer to lock it up. Instead, her profound sense of curiosity had her giving Dylan her back. She opened the manila folder and slipped out the first page of new, unwrinkled sheet music.

She shouldn't be prying. It wasn't her business. Yet she had to know. It was killing her not to know. Her hands trembling, she scanned the lyrics. "I will always love you, Janie girl." She'd forgotten he used to call her that. His Janie Girl. "Without you here, my road is bleak, my path unclear. My heart is yours without a doubt…"

Dylan cleared his throat. The innocent sound reminded her she wasn't alone. She slapped the folder shut. She'd seen enough. She didn't need to see more. What good would it do to torture herself? She was already torn up inside.

She locked the drawer before Dylan grew suspicious and turned to give him a smile. His head was still buried in the script. Then she heard the familiar sound of boots clicking down the hallway.

"Jess?"

She didn't answer. Dylan gave her a look and then called out. "We're in here, Zane. Your office."

Zane popped his head inside the doorway before entering. He shot Jess a questioning stare. She averted her eyes. She couldn't look at him right now, and he was probably wondering why she hadn't answered him. Was Zane jealous of Dylan? Did he think something was going on behind his back? It would serve him right, but that was a small consolation for her.

"Hey, Dylan. What's up?" Zane asked.

She had to get her mental bearings. She needed out of this room, pronto.

Dylan rose to shake his hand. "Hi, buddy. I came by looking for you with a new and improved version of the script. Jess invited me inside, and I was just about to go over it with her to get her opinion."

"Looks like you two don't need me now," she said. "Dylan, you can go over it with Zane. I just remembered I've got some urgent phone calls to make. See you, later."

"Sure. Later," Dylan said, distracted. He turned to his friend. "Zane, is this a good time?"

She dashed away before Zane could get any words out to the contrary. But his completely baffled expression rattled her already tightly strung nerves.

Jessica refused to shed a tear. She refused to cave to her riotous emotions. What good would it do? She'd wasted a lifetime of tears on Steven. Her well was dry. But her heart physically hurt, the kind of pain that no tears or aspirin or alcohol could cure. She marched into her room, closed the door and walked over to her bed. Plopping down, she stared out the window to majestic blue skies glazed with marshmallow tufted clouds.

She liked California. Everything was beautiful here. The people were easy, friendly and carefree. The near-tropical summer consisted of windswept days and warm, balmy nights.

But suddenly, and for the first time since coming here, she missed home. She missed her small apartment and tiny balcony where she grew cactus in a vertical garden and the jasmine flourished over the rail grating. She missed her little kitchen, her bedroom of lavender blooms and country white lace.

She missed her mama.

And her friends.

She didn't see a future with Zane. As much as it broke her heart to think it, Zane wasn't available to her emotionally. He was hung up on her sister and losing her and their baby had scarred him for life.

"You can't get blood from a stone," she muttered. It was

one of her mama's ageless comments on life. It was right up there with another Holcomb favorite: You can take a horse to water, but you can't make him drink.

Ain't that the truth?

Jessica rose and eased out of her sundress. She opened the vast walk-in closet that doubled for a black hole and selected a pair of running shoes, shorts and a top. She re-dressed quickly and lifted her long locks into a ponytail. Giving herself a glimpse in the mirror, she saw someone she didn't recognize. She'd become a California girl like the ones the Beach Boys sang about: the blonde, tanned, skimpy shorts-wearing chicks who adorned the shores of the Pacific coastline.

Jess wasn't sure how she felt about that. She wasn't sure about anything right now.

She headed down the staircase and heard male voices. There was no way to avoid Dylan and Zane since she had to walk past the office to get out the back door. She stuck her head inside the room. "Hey, guys. I'm going for a run."

Zane glanced up, but she couldn't look him in the eye, and it dawned on her in that very second, that the sick feeling invading her belly was betrayal...the lyrics of a song hurting her more than perhaps being left at the altar by the wrong man. "We're almost through here. If you wait a sec..."

"I'll join you, too," Dylan was saying.

"Uh, no thanks. I think I'll go this one alone. You guys finish up your work. I'll see you later."

She turned, but not before she saw Zane's eyes narrow to a squint, trying to figure her out.

She cringed as she walked away. She'd been border-line rude, but she couldn't help it. She needed some time alone, away from the house and the influences that could very well blindside her again. She hurried out the door and raced down the steps. She headed to where the tide teased the sand under the glorious Moonlight Beach sunshine and began to jog.

She ran at a pace that would keep her feet moving for the longest amount of time. She dodged and weaved around Frisbee-tossing teenagers, small swimsuit-clad kids digging tunnels in the wet sand and boogie boarders crashing against the shore. Sea breezes kept her cool as she dug in, jogging farther and farther away. She headed to a cove, a thin parcel of land surrounded by odd-shaped rock clusters called Moon Point that extended into the sea, forming a crescent.

The rocks looked climbable, and she was in the mood for a challenge.

Up she went, gripping the sharp edge of one rock and then finding her footing on another. Winds blew stronger here, but she held on and worked her way up. She'd heard the view from Moon Point was the best. On a clear day you could see the Santa Monica Pier. Once she got the hang of it, she was pretty good at climbing, and best of all, she was alone. She had no competition for viewing rights. She reached the top in fewer than five minutes and planted her butt on a flat part of a rock.

A hand salute kept the sun from her eyes, and she looked out at the vast ocean view. It was amazing and peaceful up here. Quiet, as if she had the entire ocean to herself.

She could stay up here all day.

Waves rocked the Point, and the sea spray sprinkled her body. The drops felt cool and refreshing, but also woke her to the time. She'd been up on the Point for three hours. She'd hardly noticed the others who'd decided to join her. They'd come and gone, but she'd stayed.

She climbed down from the rock, a deceivingly much harder proposition than going up, and she walked along the shore that was slowly and surely becoming deserted by summer school buses and mothers eager to get on the road before traffic hit. She reached the strip of beach in front of Zane's house half an hour later, and her heart somersaulted when she spotted him on the deck.

He stood with feet spread wide as if he'd been there a long time. His beige linen shirt flapped in the breeze, and his eyes, those beautiful, deep, dark eyes, locked directly on her. There was no need to wave. They'd made their connection. She stifled a whimper and headed toward him.

He started to move toward her, climbing down the steps to the sand, a loving smile absent on his lips. This was not going to be an easy conversation. For either of them.

"Where in hell did you go?" he asked.

She blinked. He'd never spoken to her in that tone. "I took a run."

"You were gone for almost four freaking hours, Jess."

"Well, I'm back now."

His bronzed face reddened to deep brick. "I can see that. Why you'd go off in such a damn hurry?"

"I needed to be alone."

"On the beach? Must've been a thousand people out today."

That was an exaggeration. "Okay, fine. I needed to get away from you for a little while."

He jerked back. "Me? What did I do? And don't change the subject. I was worried."

"Why were you worried, Zane?"

"Because, damn it. I had no idea where you were. You could've gotten swept up by a wave, or some lunatic could've grabbed you, or you might have fallen and gotten hurt. You didn't have your cell phone with you. How was I supposed to know if you were all right? Who goes jogging for four hours?"

"I needed to think."

"So, did you?"

"Yes, up on Moon Point."

Zane rolled his eyes. "You climbed the Point?"

"It wasn't hard."

The sound of teeth grinding reached her ears, but he didn't say another word.

A sigh wobbled in her throat before she released it. She laced her fingers with his and he gazed down at their hands entwined.

"Zane," she said, softening her voice. "You were worried because you care some about me, but also because you feel responsible for me. You promised my mom that you'd watch out for me. Don't deny it. I know it's true. You didn't want to fail her. I get that. I actually appreciate that. But you don't have to worry about me. I'm not the same weak, heartbroken Jess that showed up on your door more than a month ago. I've changed."

A genuine spark of sincerity flickered in his eyes. "You're amazing, Jess. Strong and smart and funny and beautiful."

She hesitated a beat. His compliments nearly destroyed her. "Don't say nice things to me."

"They're true."

"There you go again, Zane."

"Can't help it."

"I'm leaving tomorrow." She had to be strong now. She couldn't show him how her heart was cracking at this very second.

"No, you're not."

She nodded. She wouldn't be persuaded.

"What can I say to make you stay?"

She could think of a dozen things, but she remained silent.

"Why, Jess? What's happened? You owe me an explanation."

In a way, she did. "You asked what you could say to make me stay? Well, I've got something to tell you to make you rethink that."

He squeezed her hand. "Never going to happen, Jess."

"I took a pregnancy test yesterday." The words were hard to get out, and tears burned behind her eyes unexpectedly. She was through with crying. Yet one lonely drop made its way down her cheek.

Breath rushed out of his mouth. The gasp was loud enough to wake the dead. He blinked several times, staring at her as if trying to make sense of what she'd just said. His hands dropped to his sides. He probably didn't even know they had. Just like that, she had her answer.

All remnants of anger left his eyes. They filled with... fear. And he began shaking his head as if he'd heard wrong. "You took a pregnancy test?"

"Yes. I've been feeling tired and nauseated and, well, I had some other symptoms."

The fear spread to his face, which seemed to turn a putrid shade of avocado green. At any minute, he might be the one upchucking. His body, on the other hand, became one rigid piece of granite.

"I'm not pregnant."

A sigh from the depths of his chest rushed out uncontrollably fast, his breath tumbling nosily. The relief on his face drifted down to the rest of his body, and his form sagged heavily. He looked like a man who'd been given a reprieve from the worst fate in the world.

Sadly, his reaction didn't really surprise her. She'd known all along. He didn't want her child. He couldn't handle the commitment of loving another human being more than anything else in the world. He'd been there, done that once in his life. He was still plenty scarred up on the inside, but his scars also showed in his lack of commitment to his career, his floundering around, trying to reinvent himself as an actor, maybe? Or a restaurant entrepreneur. He had clipped wings, and breaking his foot had served as a means for Zane to put a temporary halt to his life.

"Maybe I shouldn't have told you," she whispered. "Kept my trap shut."

"No, no. I'm glad you did." He straightened, the gentleman and dutiful decent man that he was taking hold. But nothing could've hurt her more than seeing, *living* his response. Witnessing the somber truth in his frightened eyes for those brief moments had dissected her heart.

Yet a ridiculously hopeful part of her wished he might have been glad or even receptive to the idea of her having his child. Even if it wasn't planned. Even if it hadn't been conceived in wedlock.

When Janie had told Zane about her pregnancy, he'd been over-the-moon happy. He sent her flowers every day for a week. He hired a decorator and told her to fix up a nursery any way she wanted. He'd written a song for the baby, a soothing lullaby meant only for their new family. He'd told his friends, his fans and the press. The town of Beckon had rejoiced. Their golden boy was going to be a father.

Now Zane reclaimed her hands. His were cold and clammy, and another pang singed her heart. "I wouldn't want you to go through something like that without telling me. I, uh, want you to know that if things had turned out differently, we would've worked it out, Jess."

She didn't want to know what he meant by *working it out*. How did one work out having a baby? It didn't sound like flowers and sweet lullabies. "I know. And now you understand why I have to leave tomorrow."

She couldn't find fault with him. She knew if he could've made her feel better, he would have. But the man didn't have it in him. He didn't love her. He was through with commitment. He'd already had the one great love in his life. The stony expression on his face said it all.

A cold blast coated her insides. The frost would linger even through the Texas heat of home. She loved Zane and wanted to have his child. But he would never know her feelings. He would come to think of her as his wife's sister again.

Sweet Jess.

She wasn't destined for love.

"I'll pack my bags tonight, Zane. Don't bother to see me off. I'm leaving before dawn."

Eleven

Jessica was all about change now, moving the desks around her classroom in a new way. She wanted to see each of her students' faces when she taught in front of the blackboard. Making a connection to them was of the utmost importance. She didn't want to see their profiles but look directly into their eyes to gauge their level of attention and encourage their participation. She had her lesson plans all laid out, her mind spinning about the mark she would make on her students' lives. Who didn't remember their first-grade teacher? And she hoped they would one day think upon her fondly and know she cared.

School started in Beckon just after Labor Day, one week from today. She was eager for the semester to begin, eager to put the past behind her. Scraping sounds echoed in the classroom as she moved chairs across the linoleum floor. She was actually working up a sweat. The summer heat hadn't relented yet. September was just as hot as June in Texas.

Just minutes ago, Steven had knocked on her door. She'd been surprised to see him, but one look at his sheepish face and she knew she'd never really loved him in that forever kind of way. He'd offered her excuse after excuse and finally apologized to her. She'd listened patiently and let him have his say, all the while thinking he'd actually done her a favor by not marrying her, brutal as it had been. When he was through, it was her turn to speak. She didn't swear, didn't get angry, but calmly and very systematically gave him a piece of her mind and then dismissed him.

The new Jess had finally been heard, and it had been liberating.

She kept her hands busy maneuvering desks, not wasting another minute on Steven. But in the silence of her classroom, her mind drifted back to Zane, as it always seemed to do, and her last day in California.

Zane wouldn't let her leave on her own that morning. He'd gotten up before dawn, insisting on driving her to the airport. He had no clue how terribly hard it was for her to say goodbye. He had no way of knowing that her rebound guy had become her Mr. Right and that he'd taught her what love was truly about.

Thanks to airport regulations, Zane couldn't walk her to her boarding gate, but he'd handled her luggage and helped her get as far as he could without garnering a reprimand from security. Luckily, it was the butt crack of dawn, as her friend Sally would put it, and the Zane Williams fan club members obviously weren't early risers. Zane had told her in the car that he didn't care if he was recognized or if the paparazzi were following them—which they weren't. He wanted to see her off.

"Well," he said, dropping her luggage at his feet and taking both of her hands. His dark lashes lowered to her, framing beautiful brown eyes that seemed to give her a view into his soul. "I'll miss the hell out of you, sweetheart."

He had a way with words. The corner of her mouth lifted. How could she not love this man who'd braved Homeland Security, a possible rash of Super Fans and the ungodly early hour to wish her farewell?

"Thank you, Zane." She looked away, into the street that was starting to swarm with taxicabs and buses. She couldn't tell him she'd miss him. That would be the understatement of the century. "I appreciate you letting me stay with you. I'll miss…California."

She'd become a California girl, by Beach Boy standards.

He moved his hands up her arms, caressing her skin, and she began to prickle everywhere he touched.

"Won't you miss me a little?"

"I can't answer that, Zane." *Don't make me.*

He nodded, and his magic hands continued up her arms. "I won't ever forget the time we've spent together. It's meant a lot to me."

Her eyes squeezed shut to hold back tears. She filled her lungs, steadied herself and stared right back at him. "I won't forget, either. I'd better go. They'll be boarding soon."

"Just a sec," he said and then planted a kiss on her lips that would've brought her to her knees if he hadn't been holding her arms. He kissed her for all he was worth. And then he moved his hands to her face and cradled her cheeks, lifting her chin to position his mouth once again and stake a claim in a whopper of a kiss that brought her up onto her toes.

When the kiss ended, he pressed his forehead to hers, and they stood that way for a long time with eyes closed, their breaths mingling.

Over the loudspeaker, her flight was announced. It was time to board.

"Damn," Zane muttered and stepped back.

She lifted her luggage and began the trek that took her away from the man she loved.

He didn't ask her to stay this time.

They both knew it was over.

She had walked away from him and never did look back.

Jess shook off that memory and after accomplishing what she set out to do in the classroom, she climbed into her car and turned on the radio. Zane's melodic voice came across the airwaves. "Great, just great." She didn't need any reminders of how much she missed him. She punched off the radio and cruised along the streets of Beckon, aiming her car for home.

She needed a good soak in the tub.

Or better yet, she'd go soak her head and be done with it.

"Happy birthday, Jessica. How's my girl today?"

"Hi, Mama." Jessica left the curb in front of her apartment and bounded around the front end of her mother's car. Climbing into the passenger seat, she leaned in for a kiss. Mama planted one right smack on her cheek. The none-too-subtle scent of Elizabeth Taylor's White Diamonds perfume matched the heavy humidity in the air, but it was comforting in a way, since the classic scent defined her mama to a T. And today of all days, Jess and her mother needed the comfort.

Mama wasn't the best driver, but she insisted on picking her up and driving today. Thankfully the roads in Beckon weren't complicated or crowded, because the way her mother drove scared the daylights out of her. She clutched the steering wheel like a lifeline and rocked the darn thing from side to side with nervous jerks. Amazingly the car continued down the road in a straight line.

She looked over her shoulder at an arrangement of bubblegum-pink daylilies and snow-white roses. "Pretty flowers, Mama."

"Janie's favorites. I've got a bunch for you back at the house, sweet darlin'." It had become a ritual to visit Janie's grave on their mutual birthday. Neither of them would have it any other way.

The cemetery was on the edge of town, and it didn't take long to get there. They both stepped out of the car and walked fifty feet to the beautiful monumental headstone that Zane had had constructed. "Looks like someone's already been here today," Mama said.

More than a dozen velvety red and white roses shot up from the in-ground vase. "Zane probably had them sent." He wouldn't forget Janie's birthday. He'd always made a big deal of it when she was alive, hunting for the perfect gift for her, making her day special in any way he could.

"I don't think he had them sent," Mama said, pointing to one rose in particular. "Look at that."

"His guitar pick," Jessica said softly. Black with white lettering, the pick placed between opened petals read, "Love, Zane."

"He's in town, Jess."

"Don't be silly, Mama. Zane doesn't come here. If he was in Beckon, it'd be all over the news by now. You know how the town loves him."

"And so do you, Jessica."

"Mama," she breathed quietly. "No."

"Yes, you do. You love that man. There's no need denying it. He's a fine man, decent, and oh, boy, he loved your sister like there was no tomorrow, but Janie's gone. And Lord knows I wish she wasn't, but if you two have something—"

"Mama, I wish Janie wasn't gone. I really do, with all my heart. But you've got it wrong." She wished her sister had lived. Her baby would've been almost two by now, and she'd be the favorite aunt. Aunt Jess. Janie and Zane were meant for each other.

She was a poor substitute for the real thing.

"We'll see."

Jess ignored her mama's ominous reply and hoped that Zane wasn't within one hundred miles of Beckon. Make that one thousand.

Mama laid the flowers down, and both said a silent prayer. They stayed like usual, half an hour, talking to Janie, catching her up on news. Then, with tears welling in their eyes, said goodbye. It was always the hardest day of the year, sharing a birthday with her sister and being able to live out her birthdays while Janie's were cut short.

Mama pulled through the cemetery gates and onto the road. "How about some barbecue for your birthday dinner? I invited Sally and Louisa and Marty to join us."

Her mother, bless her soul, didn't get to grieve for Janie fully on a day that would maybe bring about some healing. Because it was Jessica's birthday as well, she had to put on a cheery front, plaster a smile on her face and pretend her heart wasn't breaking.

"Sure, Mama, that sounds good."

Sally, her best friend, and Louisa, her mama's dear friend, would be there. Marty was Louisa's daughter and also a schoolteacher. Jessica sort of got Marty's friendship by default, which was okay by her. Marty was a wonderful person.

The parking lot at BBQ Heaven was full by the time they got there. Odd for a weeknight, and though the place had new owners who'd changed the name of the restaurant from Beckon Your Bliss BBQ, it still served the best barbecue beef sliders and tri-tip in three counties. There were times back in California when she'd craved those smoky, hickory-laced meals. Now her mouth watered.

They met their friends outside and entered the place together. Seating for five wasn't a problem, it seemed. Her mama must've made reservations. They were seated at the best crescent-shaped Red Hots candy-colored booth in the restaurant. Mama and Louisa sat in the middle so they could gab, and Jessica and her friends shared the end seats.

"Thank you all for coming," Jessica said. She was getting her life back in order. Seeing Marty and Sally helped. Of course, Sally knew all. She'd picked her up from the airport when she'd returned from Moonlight Beach, and Jessica had spilled the beans. She'd sworn Sally to secrecy that day, as if they were in high school, Jess finding a way to trust a friend again. It was all good.

"Sure thing, friend. Happy birthday. Wish I was twenty-six again," Marty said with a lingering sigh.

Louisa rolled her eyes. "You're only twenty-eight, sugar."

"I know, Mom, but twenty-six was a good year for me."

Sally gave Marty a look, and all three of them laughed.

"Happy birthday, Jessica," Louisa said, her voice somber. "I hope you can find some joy today."

"I'm sure she will," Mama said with enough certainty to make Jess turn her way. Her mother's light emerald eyes were dewy soft and smiling. It was great to see her so relaxed.

The waitress came by their table. Everyone ordered a different dish for sharing, with five different sides as well, garlic mashed potatoes, white cheddar mac and cheese, bacon baked beans, almond string beans and corn soufflé. No one would go home hungry.

Bluegrass music played in the background, but no one could hear a word. The place was hopping, conversations from crowded tables going a mile a minute.

She was halfway through her salad when someone tapped on a microphone, the screeching sound check enough to bust an eardrum. Finally, the sound leveled out, the background bluegrass was history, and George, the restaurant manager, spoke into the mike. "We have a little surprise in store for you tonight," he said from the front of the room. She had to crane her neck to see him above the heads bobbing to catch a look. "Our own Zane Williams is back in town, and he's got a new song he wants to sing for all of you. Sort of a trial run, so to speak. I know not a single one of you will mind being serenaded tonight. So let's give Zane a big Beckon welcome."

Applause broke out, and just like that, Zane stepped up with a guitar strap slung over his shoulder. His six-foot-two frame, black hat and studded white shirt made him stand out from the crowd like no one else could, especially since a spotlight miraculously shone on him like a sainted cowboy who traveled with his own glow.

Lord, help her. He was amazing. She'd almost forgotten how much. And her heart did a little flip. She faced her mother who refused to look at her. And suddenly it clicked.

The innuendo at the cemetery, her mother's suspicious behavior today, the *we'll see*s and the *I'm sure she will*s.

Oh, Mama, what did you do?

Sally was beaming and mouthing, *Did you know?*

She shook her head.

And then Zane commanded his audience with simple words. "Thank y'all for letting me interrupt your meal and try out my new song on you. George, I owe you one, buddy," he said, smiling at the man standing to his side. "This one here, it's intended to wish someone I love a happy birthday. So here goes. Oh, it's called 'Janie's Song.'"

*Oh*s and *ah*s swept through the crowd. Everyone knew about Zane's undying love for Janie. A cold rash of dread kicked Jessica in the gut. Her belly ached. Bile rushed up to her mouth. How could she sit here and listen to the lyrics of the song she'd secretly read, a tribute to the love Zane still had for Janie? His voice was a beautifully rich torture instrument that would crumble her heart to powdery dust.

Her gaze darted to the door. Could she make an escape without being noticed?

Zane began to sing. Too late for an escape. He had the floor and a captivated audience. The words she'd remembered, words she'd repeated inside her head a hundred times, poured out of his mouth in a ballad pure and honest, just Zane and his guitar.

"I will always love you, Janie girl. Without you here, my road was bleak, my path unclear. My heart was yours without a doubt…"

Her mama took her hand from underneath the table and squeezed. Jessica glanced at her and found warmth brimming in her eyes. Her mother nodded toward Zane with her chin, her gaze fondly returning to him. Jessica looked down. She couldn't bear to see him sing a love song to another woman, not even to Janie. Not now, not after what they'd shared together. Was that terrible of her?

He crooned, mesmerizing everyone in the place with his

deeply wrought emotions. The pain in his voice was unmistakable, but the lyrics that filled the now quiet room were new, different, changed.

"I loved you once, and it was fine. The finest love I'd ever known. But I'm movin' on, my Janie Girl, with a love so true, I know you'd approve. You see, my girl, you love her, too. You love her, too. You love her, too. You love her, too."

Jessica snapped her head up. Zane's eyes were closed, his head tilted, his hand strumming the chords on the guitar gently as the song eased out of him. He seemed free, liberated, somehow unburdened, even as he put his heart and soul into that song.

She stared at him, unable to shift her eyes away, her mind in an uproar. When he lifted his lids, he focused on her. Only her. He removed his hat in a gallant gesture, and the dark soulful depths of his eyes reeled her in further. All heads in the restaurant turned around. Some people were gaping, others smiling. She recognized quite a few who'd attended her almost-wedding. Her face flamed. What was he doing to her?

He removed the guitar strap from his shoulder and held his instrument with one hand now. He didn't seem to care that he was making a spectacle of himself. And her.

She rose from her seat. The spotlight swiveled to her and flashed in her eyes, making her squint.

Zane took a step toward her.

Her heart was beating so fast, she thought she'd faint.

There was only one thing she could manage right now.

She bolted.

Out of the restaurant.

Into the street.

And kept on running.

"Ah, hell," Zane muttered, ignoring the applause from the crowd and granting Mae Holcomb an apologetic shrug before he took off after Jess. It hadn't gone as he'd planned, that was for doggone sure. His chin held high, he walked out of the restaurant matter-of-factly as if women ran from him every day of the week. As soon as he made it to the street, he darted his head back and forth. Once he spotted Jess nearly a half a football field away, he took off at a sprint. If Doobie Purdy, his track coach, had seen her, he would've signed her up.

But he wasn't anything if not determined, his long legs no match for her. He caught up to her in no time but slowed to a few paces behind, rethinking what he wanted to say to her. He couldn't blow it. Not again. Jess meant the world to him.

"Go away," she tossed over her shoulder.

"That's not nice." What was nice was seeing her tanned, coltish legs making strides. Lifting his gaze higher to her beautiful backside reminded him of how soft and supple she was, how amazingly gifted she was in the female department.

She didn't slow her pace, not for a second.

"Ouch, damn it. I hurt my foot," Zane yelped.

She stopped then and turned, her eyes focused on his fake injury. He saw the depth of her compassion, the love she had for him glowing in her eyes—Dylan hadn't been wrong—and loved her so damn much right now, he could hardly breathe.

"You're not hurt, are you?"

"My heart is bleeding."

She gasped. A good sign.

"But your foot is fine, right?" She stared at his feet.

"Well, my foot could be hurt, Jess. Running like a bat outta hell to catch you in these boots isn't the kind of therapy I need."

She shook her head, and the gorgeous mass of blonde hair curled around her face. The run had put a rosy blush on her face, and the material of her coral dress lifted her ample chest with every breath she took, nearly killing him.

He inhaled now and was grateful she wasn't moving again. "You *really* don't play fair, Zane."

"I needed to see you today. On your birthday."

"Zane, what were you thinking? You made a spectacle of me in that restaurant. You of all people know I don't need another scandal in my life. I've had enough of being the laughingstock in this town. I… Why are you really here?"

"I came for you."

Hope popped into her eyes. Another good sign.

"You changed the words of the song."

"Dylan said he thought you'd seen those lyrics. He was right, wasn't he? Is that why you wouldn't stay with me?"

"Dylan? Are you taking advice from the Casanova now?"

"Don't knock Dylan. He's the one who made me see how much I missed you. How stupid I've been. And yes, after you left, I reworked the song, the lyrics coming easy and straight outta my heart. I sang it tonight just for you."

She folded her arms, and a warm glint entered her eyes. "But why there, in front of half the town?"

"I let you go. I was running scared. When you told me you might've been carrying my child, I couldn't deal with it, Jess. I've been blaming myself for Janie's death all this time, feeling guilty about losing her and our child. Deep down, I hated myself. I didn't think I'd ever want again, or love again. It was easier to live in the moment and not look to the future. But then you left, and I was hollowed out, gutted to my sorry bones. I missed you something fierce. I didn't think me saying it would be enough. I didn't know if you'd believe me unless I shouted it from the rooftops.

"I'm not doing the movie, and the restaurant is the last one I'm building. I'm going to finish up my tour, Jess. I'm through hiding my head in the sand. I'm through not being me."

The corners of her mouth lifted. He wanted to see her pretty smile again, but it wasn't there, not yet. "That's good, Zane. I'm happy for you."

Cars swerved around them. Someone honked a horn. Zane took her hand and guided her out of the middle of the street, to the sidewalk in front of the Cinema Palace. Ironically, it was nearly the same spot where he'd fallen in love with Janie. And now, here he was coming full circle, praying that her sister would agree to spend her life with him.

"Do you love me, Jess?"

She stared at him as if he were a three-headed monster. "Do you?"

She pulled her hands free of him. "Yes, you idiot."

His face split wide open, and he didn't care if he looked like a grinning fool. Joy rushed out so fast he couldn't stop himself from telling her his plans. "I'm selling off my place, Jess. Finally. The land where I lived with your sister will belong to someone else one day soon. I'll never forget Janie, but it's time to move on. There's this beautiful parcel of land I've got my eye on. But I want you to see it, too. I want you to love it as much as I do. I'm digging in and putting down roots again, here in Beckon."

"But you said you're going back on tour."

"I have to finish it up. I'm bound by the contract, but after that, Jess, I'll stay here in Beckon and tour only during the summer months, when you're not teaching."

The smile he was praying for was almost there. "Zane, what are you saying?"

"Oh, yeah, got ahead of myself, didn't I?" He inhaled deeply and took hold of her hands. "I've already spoken to your mama, Jess. She and I worked things out, and she's given me her blessing. Sweet Jess, my Jess, you've helped me heal my body and my heart. And I can't imagine my life without you. Jessica Holcomb, I'm getting down on one knee," he said, his knee hitting the pavement. He tilted his head up and gazed into her eyes. "You taught me to look toward the future again. Knowing you, loving you the way I do, has given me the courage I needed to find my true self. I'm not afraid anymore. And I'm asking you for a second chance. I'm asking you to share your life with me. I'm asking you to be my wife, Jess. And Lord knows, have my baby one day. I want that. I really do. I love you with all my heart. Will you marry me, sweet Jess?"

Her beautiful, soft, grass-green eyes teared up, but her smile was real and genuine and the most beautiful thing about her. She hesitated so long he thought he'd blown it, but then she pulled him up and he stood facing her, his heart in her hands. "No girl marries her rebound guy," she said, her smile widening. "But me. I love you, Zane. I want to be your wife and spend the rest of my life with you."

"I'm so happy you said yes. 'Cause I wasn't gonna take no for an answer. It's all sorta weird and wonderful and unexpected, sweetheart, but my love is true. You have to know that."

"I do. And I think just like you said in your song, Janie would approve. She's looking down on us now and giving her blessing, too."

Holcomb women sure had a hold on him. "I'd love to believe so."

"I believe it, Zane. Let's go back to the restaurant and share our good news. Mama looked worried when I walked out."

"She wasn't the only one." Zane took her into his arms and pressed a kiss onto her soft, sweet lips. Planting his stake, claiming his woman. He was gonna hold on tight and never let her go.

Ever again.

* * * * *

Available March 3, 2015

#2359 ROYAL HEIRS REQUIRED
Billionaires and Babies • by Cat Schield
Love and duty collide as Prince Gabriel Alessandro weds Lady Olivia Darcy to assume his nation's throne. But when he discovers he's the secret father of twin girls, will all bets be off?

#2360 MORE THAN A CONVENIENT BRIDE
Texas Cattleman's Club: After the Storm
by Michelle Celmer
What could be simpler than a marriage of convenience between friends? That's what star Texas surgeon Lucas Wakefield and researcher Julie Kingston think, until a jealous ex shows up and throws a wrench in their plans.

#2361 AT THE RANCHER'S REQUEST
Lone Star Legends • by Sara Orwig
It was a dark and stormy night when billionaire rancher Mike Calhoun rescued the stranded motorist. Now the widower has a storm in his own life as he's torn by unwanted attraction to this pregnant, vulnerable beauty...

#2362 AFTER HOURS WITH HER EX
by Maureen Child
When prodigal son Sam Wyatt comes home to his family's ski resort, he must work with his estranged wife to keep the business alive. But does this mean new life for the relationship he left behind?

#2363 PREGNANT BY THE SHEIKH
The Billionaires of Black Castle • by Olivia Gates
Numair can reclaim his birthright and gain the power of two thrones by marrying Jenan. And Jenan is more than willing to provide an heir for this delicious man—until she discovers his true agenda.

#2364 THE WEDDING BARGAIN
The Master Vintners • by Yvonne Lindsay
Shanal will sacrifice everything, even wed her unlovable boss, for her destitute parents' sakes. But when she gets cold feet at the altar, it's white knight Raif to the rescue. Will their desire be her redemption?

YOU CAN FIND MORE INFORMATION ON UPCOMING HARLEQUIN® TITLES, FREE EXCERPTS AND MORE AT WWW.HARLEQUIN.COM.

REQUEST YOUR FREE BOOKS!
2 FREE NOVELS PLUS 2 FREE GIFTS!

HARLEQUIN®

Desire

ALWAYS POWERFUL, PASSIONATE AND PROVOCATIVE

HD13R

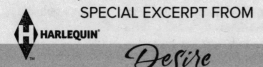
"We'll have to kiss," she heard Luc say, and it took her
brain a second to catch up with her ears.

"Kiss?"

"During the wedding ceremony," he said.

"Oh, right." Julie hadn't considered that. She thought
about kissing Luc, and a peculiar little shiver cascaded
down the length of her spine. Back when she'd first met
him, she used to think about the two of them doing a lot
more than just kissing, but he had been too hung up on
Amelia and their recently broken engagement to even
think about another woman. So hung up that he'd left
his life in Royal behind and traveled halfway around the
world with Doctors Without Borders.

A recent dumpee herself, Julie had been just as confused and vulnerable at the time, and she'd known there
would be nothing worse for her ego than a rebound

relationship. She and Luc were, and always would be, better off as friends.

"Is that a problem?" Luc asked.

She blinked. "Problem?"

"Us kissing. You got an odd look on your face."

Had she? "It's no problem at all," she assured him.

"We'll have to start acting like a married couple," he said. "You'll have to move in with me. But nothing in our relationship will change. We only have to make it look as if it has."

But by pretending, by making it look real to everyone else, wasn't that in itself a change to their relationship?

Ugh. She'd never realized how complicated this would be.

"Look," he said, frowning. "I want you to stay in the US, but if it's going to cause a rift in our friendship... Do you think it's worth it?"

"It is worth it. And I don't want you to think that I'm not grateful. I am."

"I know you are." He smiled and laid a hand on her forearm, and the feel of his skin against hers gave her that little shiver again.

What the heck was going on between them?

Don't miss
MORE THAN A CONVENIENT BRIDE
by Michelle Celmer, available March 2015 wherever
Harlequin® Desire books and ebooks are sold.

www.Harlequin.com

JUST CAN'T GET ENOUGH
ROMANCE
Looking for more?

Harlequin has everything from contemporary, passionate and heartwarming to suspenseful and inspirational stories.

Whatever your mood, we have a romance just for you!

Connect with us to find your next great read, special offers and more.

Facebook.com/HarlequinBooks
Twitter.com/HarlequinBooks
HarlequinBlog.com
Harlequin.com/Newsletters

HARLEQUIN®

A *Romance* FOR EVERY MOOD™

www.Harlequin.com